# GOLDEN GARRISONS LOSING THEIR TOUCH?

The rumor mill is working overtime this week, folks! Sources inside the Garrison Grand have informed us that Mrs. Bonita Garrison will be celebrating her sixtieth birthday at a room in the super swanky Estate nightclub, owned by her son Adam. No word on whether Mama Garrison will be able to stand upright at her own celebration, as we hear she has no intentions of drying herself out for the upcoming gala.

We've also heard that Jordan Jefferies, rival of family head honcho Parker Garrison, snagged a lucrative real-estate deal from the competition. First, Hotel Victoria—guaranteed to steal the cream of the crop clientele from the Garrison Grand when it opens next season. Then, the alleged acquisition of former fully-owned Garrison property Brittany Beach. Now this. Seems like the Garrisons may be losing their touch.

Dear Reader,

I hope you are enjoying the stories in the Silhouette Desire series, THE GARRISONS. I enjoyed working closely with the other five authors to bring you a scintillating tale of a family's hidden secrets, skyrocketing passion and endless love.

In my story, Brandon Washington was a man with a plan…or so he thought. Until he meets the heroine, Cassie Sinclair-Garrison. Then he finds out the hard way that no matter what your intentions are, when emotions get in the way even the best-laid plans can get kicked to the curb.

I love writing romance stories in which the hero and heroine are pitted against each other, but in the end, true love prevails.

I hope you enjoy Brandon and Cassie's story and their journey to finding everlasting love.

Best,

*Brenda Jackson*

# BRENDA JACKSON

## STRANDED WITH THE TEMPTING STRANGER

*Silhouette®*

*Desire*

Published by Silhouette Books

**America's Publisher of Contemporary Romance**

To Gerald Jackson, Sr.
Thank you for 35 years of love and romance.
To my Heavenly Father for giving me the gift to write.
My beloved *is* mine, and I *am* his: he feedeth among the lilies.
*Song of Solomon* 2:16 II
Special thanks and acknowledgment are given to Brenda Jackson
for her contribution to THE GARRISONS miniseries.

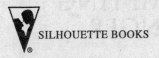

SILHOUETTE BOOKS

ISBN-13: 978-0-373-76825-7
ISBN-10:    0-373-76825-7

STRANDED WITH THE TEMPTING STRANGER

Visit Silhouette Books at www.eHarlequin.com

**Printed in U.S.A.**

**Books by Brenda Jackson**

Silhouette Desire

*Delaney's Desert Sheikh* #1473
*A Little Dare* #1533
*Thorn's Challenge* #1552
Scandal Between the Sheets #1573
*Stone Cold Surrender* #1601
*Riding the Storm* #1625
*Jared's Counterfeit Fiancée* #1654
Strictly Confidential Attraction #1677
Taking Care of Business #1705
*The Chase Is On* #1690
*The Durango Affair* #1727
*Ian's Ultimate Gamble* #1756
*Seduction, Westmoreland Style* #1778
Stranded with the Tempting Stranger #1825

*Westmoreland family titles

Kimani Romance

Solid Soul #1
Night Heat #19
Risky Pleasures #37
In Bed with the Boss #53

---

## BRENDA JACKSON

is a die "heart" romantic who married her childhood sweetheart and still proudly wears the going steady ring he gave her when she was fifteen. Because she's always believed in the power of love, Brenda's stories always have happy endings. In her real-life love story, Brenda and her husband live in Jacksonville, Florida, and have two sons.

A *USA TODAY* bestselling author, Brenda divides her time between family, writing and working in management at a major insurance company. You may write Brenda at P.O. Box 28267, Jacksonville, FL 32226, by e-mail at WriterBJackson@aol.com or visit her Web site at www.brendajackson.net.

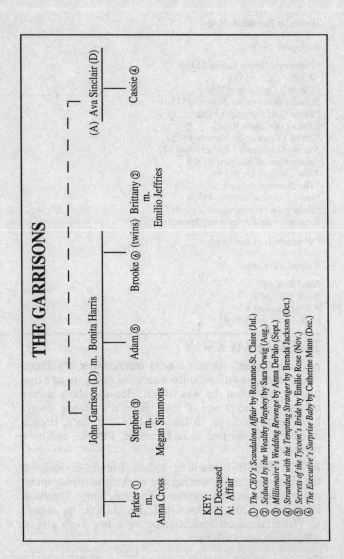

# THE GARRISONS

John Garrison (D) m. Bonita Harris ---- (A) Ava Sinclair (D)

Parker ① — Stephen ③ — Adam ⑤ — Brooke ⑥ (twins) Brittany ② — Cassie ④
m.        m.                        m.
Anna Cross   Megan Simmons                    Emilio Jeffries

KEY:
D: Deceased
A: Affair

① *The CEO's Scandalous Affair* by Roxanne St. Claire (Jul.)
② *Seduced by the Wealthy Playboy* by Sara Orwig (Aug.)
③ *Millionaire's Wedding Revenge* by Anna DePalo (Sept.)
④ *Stranded with the Tempting Stranger* by Brenda Jackson (Oct.)
⑤ *Secrets of the Tycoon's Bride* by Emilie Rose (Nov.)
⑥ *The Executive's Surprise Baby* by Catherine Mann (Dec.)

# One

Cassie Sinclair-Garrison released an uneven breath when she rounded the corner in the lobby of her hotel. She stopped, totally mesmerized by the man standing at the counter to check in to the Garrison Grand-Bahamas. It had been a long time since any man had captured her attention like this one. He was simply gorgeous.

He stood tall at a height of not less than six-three with an athletic build that indicated he was a sportsman or someone who made it his business to stay in great physical shape. He was an American, she knew at once, studying his coffee-brown skin, his dark brown eyes and closely shaved head. And he wasn't here on business, she thought, noting the way he was immaculately dressed in a pair of dark brown trousers and a tan shirt that brought out the beautiful coloring of his skin.

She didn't know what, but there was something about him that demanded attention and from the way other women in the lobby were also staring, it was attention he was definitely getting.

Deciding she had more to do with her time than to practically drool over a man, Cassie pushed the button to the elevator that would take her to her office on the executive floor. It was an office that once belonged to her father.

Five years ago, when she was twenty-two, her father had made her manager and there hadn't been a time when he hadn't been pleased with the way she had handled things. That's why she wasn't surprised that upon his death he had left full ownership of the hotel to her. In doing so he had only confirmed what some of her employees had probably suspected all along—that she was John Garrison's illegitimate child.

A flutter of pain touched her heart as she thought of her parents. She stepped inside the elevator, glad it was vacant because whenever she encountered these types of moments, she preferred being alone. Although she had tried putting on a good front over the past five months, it had been hard to first lose her mother in an auto accident and, little over a month later, lose her father when he'd died of a heart attack…although it was probably more of a broken heart.

She had wondered how he would be able to go on after her mother's death. The last time she had seen her father—just days before he passed when he had come to visit her—Cassie had seen the depths of pain in his eyes and she had wondered how he would get over the loss. He had said more than once that losing his Ava was like losing a part of him.

Even though he was a married man that hadn't stopped him from falling in love with her mother, the beautiful and vivacious Ava Sinclair. And she had been John Garrison's true love for more than twenty-eight years.

According to her mother, she had met the wealthy and very handsome American in the States when he had been a judge and she a contestant in the Miss Universe beauty pageant as Miss Bahamas. Their paths had crossed a few years later, when he had visited the Bahamas to purchase land for this grand hotel he intended to build.

Although he had a family in Florida consisting of five kids, he was an unhappy man, a man who was no longer in love with his wife, but too dedicated to his children to walk away from his marriage.

Cassie hadn't understood their relationship until she was older, but it was beyond clear her parents had shared something special, something unique and something few people had. It was a love of a lifetime. Ava never made any demands on John, yet he had freely lavished her with anything and everything, and provided her and the child they had created with complete financial support.

Cassie knew that others who'd seen her parents together over the years had formed opinions on what the relationship was about. He was a married American and Ava was his Bahamian mistress. But Cassie knew their relationship was so much more than that. In her heart she believed they had been soul mates in the truest form. She had loved her parents deeply and they had loved her, a product of their love, and there hadn't been a day they hadn't let her feel or know it.

She had resented those times when her father would leave them to return to his family in Miami, a family she'd only found out about when she became a teenager. The truth had hurt, but then her mother and father had smoothed away the pain with the intensity of their love and had let her know that no matter what the situation was, the one thing that would never change or diminish was their love for her, as well as their love for each other. From that day forward, whether others did or not, Cassie understood and accepted her parents' unorthodox love affair.

She stepped off the elevator and walked into her office, stopping to smile at her secretary while picking up her messages off the woman's desk. "Good morning, Trudy."

"Good morning, Ms. Garrison."

Cassie liked the sound of that. She had begun using her father's last name within a week of his death. With both of her parents deceased, there were no secrets to protect and she had no reason to continue to deny herself the use of his name.

"Any additional messages?" she asked the older woman whom she had hired a few months ago.

"Yes. Mr. Parker Garrison just called and would like you to return his call."

Cassie forced the smile to stay on her face while thinking that no matter what Parker liked, he wouldn't

be getting things his way since she wouldn't be returning his call. She could not forget the phone conversation
they had shared nearly four months ago. He'd called
within a week of the reading of John Garrison's will and
he'd kept calling. Eventually, she had taken his call.

At the time she had been very aware that he, his
siblings and mother had been shocked to discover at
the reading of the will that John Garrison had an
outside child. Of the five Garrison offspring, Parker
had been the most livid because the terms of their
father's will gave her and Parker equal controlling
interest in Garrison Inc., an umbrella corporation that
oversaw the stocks and financial growth of all the
Garrison-owned properties. He wasn't happy about it.

Their telephone conversation hadn't gone well. He
had been arrogant, condescending and had even tried
being intimidating. When he'd seen Cassie would not
accept his offer to buy her out, he had done the un-
thinkable by saying she had to prove she was a Garrison,
and had threatened her with a DNA test as well as the
possibility of him contesting the will. Parker's threats
had ticked her off and she was still angry.

"Ms. Garrison?"

Her secretary's voice recaptured her attention. The
forced smile widened. "Thank you for delivering the
message."

Cassie entered her office. She would think Parker
would have more to do with his time these days. It didn't
take long for news to travel over the hotel grapevine that
the handsome and elusive playboy had gotten married.
And not that she cared, but she'd also heard that another
Garrison bachelor, Stephen, had gotten hitched, as well.

She had no intention of ever meeting any of her "siblings." She didn't know them and they didn't know her and she preferred things stayed that way. They had never been a part of her life and she had never been a part of theirs. She had a life here in the Bahamas and saw no need to change that.

As she sat behind her desk her thoughts shifted back to the guy she'd seen in the lobby. She couldn't help but wonder if he was married or single, straight or gay. She shrugged her shoulders knowing that it really didn't matter. The last thing she needed was to become interested in a man. Her man was the beautiful thirty-story building that was erected along the pristine shoreline of the Caribbean. And "her man" was a beautiful sight that took her breath away each time she entered his lobby. And she would take care of him, continue to make him prosper the way her father would want her to do. Now that her parents were gone, this hotel was the only thing she could depend on for happiness.

Brandon Washington glanced around the room he had been given, truly impressed. He had spent plenty of time at the Garrison Grand but there was something about this particular franchise that left him astonished. It was definitely a tropical paradise.

The first thing he'd noticed when he had pulled into the parking lot was that the structure was different from the sister hotel in South Miami Beach, mainly because it was designed to take advantage of the tropical island beach it sat on. And it was nested intimately among a haven of palm trees and a multitude

of magnificent gardens that were stocked with flow-
ering plants.

The second was the warmth of the staff that had
greeted him the moment he had walked into the beautiful atrium. They had immediately made him feel
welcome and important.

And then it was his hotel room, a beautiful suite with
a French balcony that looked out at the ocean. It had to
be the most stunning waterscape view he'd ever seen.

Brandon was more than pleased with his accommo-
dations. And since he planned to stay for a while, his
comfort was of the utmost importance. He had to
remind himself that this was not a vacation, but he'd
come here with a job to do. He needed to uncover any
secrets Cassie Sinclair-Garrison might have that could
be used to persuade her to give up her controlling
interest in Garrison, Inc., his most influential client.
Not to mention that members of the family were close
friends of his.

His father had been John Garrison's college friend
and later his personal attorney for over forty years and
Brandon had been a partner in his father's law firm.
When his father was killed in a car accident three years
ago, instead of transferring the Garrison business to a
more experienced and older attorney, John had
retained Brandon's firm, showing his loyalty to the
Washington family and his faith in Brandon's abilities.

Brandon had known John Garrison all of his thirty-
two years and he was a man Brandon had respected.
And he considered Adam Garrison, one of John's sons,
his very best friend. Now Brandon was here at the
request of Parker and Stephen Garrison. It seemed

John's illegitimate daughter refused to deal with the corporation in any way and had refused to discuss any type of a buyout offer with Parker.

Before resorting to a full-blown court battle, the two eldest brothers had suggested that Brandon travel to the Bahamas, assume a false identity to see if he could get close to Ms. Garrison and dig up any information on her present or her past, which would give them ammunition to later force her hand if she continued to refuse to sell her shares of Garrison, Inc. Another smart thing John had done was retain exclusive control of this particular hotel, the one Cassie had managed and now owned. No doubt it had been a brainy strategic move to keep his secrets well-hidden.

Brandon pulled his cell phone from his coat jacket when it rang. "Yes?"

A smile touched his lips. "Yes, Parker, I just checked in and just so you'll know, I'm registered under the name of Brandon Jarrett."

He chuckled. "That's right. I'm using my first and middle name since I want to keep my real identity hidden." A few moments later he ended his phone call with Parker.

Brandon began unpacking. He had brought an assortment of casual clothes since it was his intent to pose as a businessman who'd come to the island for a short but very needed vacation. That shouldn't be hard to do, because since John Garrison's death and his secrets had been revealed, Brandon had been working long hours with the Garrison family to resolve all the unwanted issues.

Contesting the will had been out of the question. No

one wanted to air the family's dirty laundry. Doing so would definitely send John's widow, Bonita, over the edge. There were a number of people who would not sympathize with the woman, saying it was her drinking problem that had sent John into the arms of another woman in the first place and that he had stayed married to her longer than most men would have.

Then there would be others who would think that John's extramarital affair is what had driven the woman to drink. As far as Brandon was concerned, there was no way Bonita hadn't known about John's affair, given the amount of time he spent away from home. But from the look on her face during the reading of the will, she had not known a child had been involved. Now she knew, and according to Adam, his mother was hitting the bottle more than ever.

Brandon rubbed his chin, feeling the need of a shave. As he continued to unpack he knew that sometime within the next couple of days he would eventually cross paths with Cassie Sinclair-Garrison. He would make sure of it.

Cassie stood on one of the many terraces on the east side of the hotel, which faced Tahita Bay. It was late afternoon yet the sky was still a dazzling blue and seemed to match the waters beneath it. There were a number of yachts in the bay and several human bodies were sunbathing on the beach.

She smiled and waved her hand when a couple she'd met yesterday when they'd checked in recognized her and gave her a greeting as they glided by on a sailboat. At least she had met the woman yesterday; the man she already knew from the numerous times when his family's corporation—Elliott Publishing Holdings; one of the largest magazine conglomerates in the world—had utilized the hotel to host their annual business conference. Their main office was located in New York and the Garrison Grand-Bahamas was the ideal place to hold a seminar during the winter months.

Teagan Elliott was here vacationing with his wife of eight months, a beautiful African-American by the name of Renee. An interracial couple, the two looked very good together and reminded Cassie of what she thought every time she would see her parents together. And just like her parents, it was easy to see their love was genuine.

Thinking of her parents sent a feeling of forlornness through her. Now that the business of the day had been handled, she decided to stay at the hotel for the night instead of taking the thirty-minute drive to her home, which was located on the other side of the island. Maybe later she'd take a leisurely stroll along the shoreline in an area that wasn't so crowded.

She thought of the Diamond Keys, an exclusive section of the hotel that had beachfront suites with parlors and French doors that opened directly to the water, providing a commanding view of endless beach and ocean. The rooms, which were extremely expensive but definitely worth it, were nestled in the hotel's most intimate settings.

Cassie headed back inside, making her way to her bedroom to change out of her business suit and slip into a pair of silk lounging pants and matching camisole with a print design. It had been a long time since she'd carved out some time for herself. Over the past months she had spent the majority of her time wallowing in work and mourning the loss of her parents, as she tried to move on through life, one day at a time.

She had been at her mother's funeral, standing beside her father, who'd remained in shock over their unexpected loss. What hurt so much even now was that she hadn't attended her father's funeral. By the time she had received word of his death, the funeral had already taken place. All she had was the memory of the last time they had spent together, a few days before his death.

He had shown up on the island unexpectedly, not at the hotel but at her condo, waiting for her when she had arrived home from work that day. The handsome and charismatic man she'd always known and loved had held sadness in his eyes and pain in his features.

That night he had taken her out to dinner and before he had returned to Miami, he had placed in her hand the deed to the beautiful ten-acre estate in the exclusive Lyford Cay community that he had purchased for her mother fifteen years ago. It was the home she now occupied and called her own.

Cassie took a glance around as she stepped out onto the sandy shores. Daylight had faded and dusk had set in. But that didn't bother her. In fact she much preferred it. She always thought the beach at night was breathtakingly beautiful. In the background she heard the band from the lounge as it mixed with the sound of the waves crashing against the shore. She leaned down and took off her sandals, wanting to feel the sand beneath her feet. Being on the beach always made her feel better. It helped her momentarily forget her pain, and made her feel carefree, energized and invigorated.

She bit back a smile and glanced around again, just to make sure she was alone, before pretending to play hopscotch on the sand. She laughed out loud when she almost slipped as she continued to hop around on one foot from one pretend square block to another. What a wonderful way to work off the day's stress, she thought, and today had definitely been a busy one. The hotel's capacity was at an all-time high, with requests for extended stays becoming the norm. They even had a waiting list for weeks not considered as prime time. The man she had chosen to succeed her as a manager, Simon Tillman, was doing an excellent job, and now she was able to concentrate on doing other things, such as expanding her business in various ways.

She had received a call from her accountant that profits for the hotel were surging. Once it had become official that she was the owner of the Garrison Grand-Bahamas, she had begun implementing the changes she had submitted to her father in a proposal just a month before his death. Over the last dinner they had shared together, he had given his blessing to move ahead with her plans. Today after meeting with her staff, she had a lot to be happy about, for the first time in months.

"May I play?"

Cassie lowered her leg as she swung around at the sound of the deep, masculine voice, angry at the intrusion. She narrowed her eyes, at first not seeing anyone, but then she watched as a man seemed to materialize out of the darkness.

She recognized him immediately. He was the man

she had seen earlier today when he had checked into the hotel. He was the man every woman in the hotel had been watching, and a man who even now was taking her breath away.

her then eat her with anomaly how in and asked out and
the Doris fixed was the sin but reliving brought he board
ajar went get building and want a stay with some and
coming both only ever

# Two

Brandon stared at the woman standing a few feet from him. He had been watching her, barely seeing her features in the shadows, and now with her standing so close, he thought she had to be the most beautiful woman he had ever seen. He immediately wanted to know everything about her.

He glanced at her left hand, didn't see a ring and inwardly let out a relieved breath. But that didn't necessarily mean she didn't have a significant other, even perhaps a boyfriend. What were the chances of her spending time at this hotel, one known for rest, relaxation and romance, alone?

But still, that didn't stop his hormones from going into overdrive when he stared into her face, seeing the cocoa color of her complexion, the dark curly brown hair that fell to her shoulders, the darkness of her brown eyes and the shape of her curves in the outfit she was wearing.

Disgusted, he was reminded of why he was there, which was not to concentrate on a woman whose looks were so striking they could almost blind him, but to get close to a woman who was causing problems to his biggest client—a woman he had yet to meet, although he'd hung around the hotel the majority of the day hoping that he would. When he had discreetly asked about her, he'd been told that Cassie Sinclair-Garrison had been in meetings all day and chances were she had already left for her home, which was on the other side of the island.

In that case, since it wasn't likely he would be running into Ms. Garrison anytime tonight, why not spend time with this beauty...if she was free and available.

He watched how she tilted up her chin and narrowed her eyes at him. "You intrude on my privacy."

Her Bahamian accent was rich, just as rich as the curly brown hair that flowed around her shoulders, he thought. With the lifting of her chin he zeroed in on more of her features. In addition to her creamy brown skin, she had high cheekbones, a cute dimple in her chin, a straight nose and lips so full and generous they were downright sexy. There was something so feminine about her it actually made him ache.

"And I apologize," he said quietly, accepting what she felt was her need to take him to task. "I was out for a walk and couldn't help but notice the game you were playing. "

"You could have said something to let me know you were there," she said directly, eyeing him.

"And you're right, but again, I got so caught up in watching you that I didn't want to interrupt, at least not for a while. If I upset you, I'm sorry."

Cassie realized she really shouldn't make such a big deal out of it. After all it wasn't just her section of private beach, but belonged to anyone who was staying at Diamond Keys, and evidently he was. "Since there hasn't been any harm done," she said in a muffled voice, "I will accept your apology."

He smiled. "Thank you. And I hope you will let me make it up to you."

"And how do you pose to do that?"

"By asking you to be my guest at dinner tonight," he said lightly, watching the look of surprise skim her features at his request.

She shook her head. "That's not necessary."

"I think it is. I offended you and want to make it up to you."

"You didn't offend me. You just caught me off guard."

"Still, I'd like to make it up to you."

Cassie bent her head, trying to hide the smile that suddenly touched her lips. If nothing else, he was persistent. Shouldn't she be as persistent, as well, in turning down his offer?

She lifted her head and met his gaze and for a period of time she was rendered speechless. He had moved into into her line of vision and she thought he was so incredibly handsome, she could actually feel a rush of blood flow through her veins. She doubted that very few women turned down anything coming from him.

"Maybe we should introduce ourselves," he said,

taking a step forward and smiling. He extended his hand out to her. "I'm Brandon Jarrett."

"And I'm Cassie Sinclair-Garrison."

It took everything Brandon had to keep the shock that rocked his body from showing in his face. This was Cassie Garrison? The woman who was causing Garrison, Inc., all kinds of trouble? The woman who had been giving Parker heartburn for the past four months? The woman who was a sibling to the Miami Garrisons whether she wanted to acknowledge them or not? The woman who was the main reason he was here on the island?

"Hello, Cassie Sinclair-Garrison," he said, forcing the words out of his mouth and hesitantly releasing her hand. It had felt good in his, as if it had actually belonged there. He had looked forward to meeting Cassie, but without this element of surprise. He didn't like surprises and this one was a biggie.

"Hello, Brandon Jarrett," she said, smiling. "I hope you're enjoying your stay here."

"I am. Are you?" he asked, not wanting to give anything away that he recognized her name or knew who she was, although she carried the same last name as the hotel.

"Yes, I'm enjoying myself."

No doubt at my expense, he thought, when he saw she had no intention of mentioning that she was the hotel's owner. "I think you might enjoy it even more if you have dinner with me."

A feeling of uneasiness crept over Cassie. The moment her fingers had slid into the warmth of his when they had shaken hands, she had felt a surge of sensations that settled in the middle of stomach. This guy was smooth and the problem was that she wasn't used to smooth guys. She dated, but not frequently, and definitely not someone like Brandon Jarrett. It was quite obvious he knew how to work *it* and it was also quite obvious that he thought he had a chance of working her. That realization didn't repulse her like it should have. Instead it had her curious. He wouldn't be the first man who'd tried hitting on her, but he was the first who had remotely triggered her interest in over a year or so.

"We're back to that, are we?" she asked, chuckling, feeling a little more relaxed than she had earlier.

"Yes, I'm afraid we're back to that, and I hope you don't disappoint me. We can dine here at the hotel or go someplace else that's close by. It will be your choice."

She knew if would be crazy to suggest to a perfect stranger to take her someplace other than here, but the last thing she wanted was to become the topic of conversation of her employees. Some of them hadn't yet gotten over the shock that John Garrison was her biological father and that he had left the hotel to her. Making a decision she hoped that she didn't later regret she said, "I prefer going someplace else that's close by."

She could tell her response pleased him. "Is there any place you want to recommend or do you prefer leaving the choice to me?" he asked.

Again putting more trust in him than she really should, she said, "I'll leave things to you."

"All right. Do you want us to meet in the lobby in about an hour?"

She knew that wouldn't work. "No, we can meet

back here, at least over there on that terrace near the flower garden."

"Okay."

If he found her request strange he didn't let on. "Then I'll see you back here in an hour, Cassie Sinclair-Garrison," he said, smiling again.

Her heart missed a beat with his smile and, holding his gaze a bit longer than she should have, she said goodbye and then turned and quickly began walking back across the sand to her suite.

As Brandon headed back toward his room, he felt more than the October breeze off the ocean. A rush of adrenaline was pumping fast and furious through his veins. What were the chances of the one woman he had been attracted to since his breakup with Jamie Frigate a year ago to be the woman he had purposely come here to get to know?

*Jamie.*

Even now he had to steel himself against the rising anger he always felt when he thought about his fiancée's betrayal. How any woman could have been so shallow and full of herself he would never know. But more than that, she had been greedy as hell. She hadn't been satisfied with just having the things he could give her. While engaged to him she'd had an affair with a California businessman. He had found out about her duplicity when he had returned to Miami unexpectedly from a work-related trip to find her in bed with the man.

He entered his suite, not wanting to think about Jamie any longer, and instead his thoughts shifted back to Cassie. Any information he shared about himself to her would basically be false. But under the circumstances, that couldn't be helped. Tonight things had fallen into place too nicely for him and for some reason he was bothered by it. The woman he had seen playing a game of hopscotch had had an innocent air about her, definitely not what he had expected. And he had detected some sort of vulnerability, as well.

And he couldn't dismiss just how incredibly beautiful she was. With her striking good looks he would think she would have a date every night of the week. So the question that was presently popping in his mind was why didn't she?

In just the brief time he had spent with Cassie he had a feeling she was extremely bright. Maybe it had been the way she had studied him before making the decision to join him for dinner tonight that had given him that perspective.

A chuckle welled up inside of Brandon. He would find out just how bright she was at dinner when he really got into the game of wining and dining her. Whatever it took, he needed her to feel comfortable enough with him to share things about herself; things that could possibly damage her reputation if they became public knowledge.

He was suddenly unnerved by what he had to do and if he dwelled on it too long he would probably find the entire thing disgusting. But he could not let personal feelings or emotions intervene. He had a job to do and he intended to do it well.

Cassie glanced at herself in the mirror once more. She had taken another shower and changed outfits.

This one was a dress her mother had bought her earlier in the year that she had never worn until tonight.

It was a slinky thin-strapped mini-dress, fuchsia in color, and what made it elegant was the silver-clasp tie neck. She nervously smoothed the dress down her body, wondering if perhaps in trying to make a good impression she was making some sort of a statement, as well.

She ran her fingers though the long, dark brown curls on her head, fluffing them around her face. A face she thought had a remarkable resemblance to both of her parents, but mainly her father. She had her mother's eyes but her father's mouth, nose and cheekbones. And then there was that cleft in her chin that definitely came from him.

Her skin coloring was a mixture of the both of them, but her smile was that of John Garrison. She chewed her bottom lip nervously, thinking her smile was something she hadn't shown much of lately. But tonight she had smiled more than once already, although she had lowered her head so Brandon wouldn't see it the first time she'd done so.

She inhaled deeply, thinking for the umpteenth time that Brandon Jarrett was so drop-dead gorgeous it was a shame. No man should be walking around looking like he did and with a well-toned muscled body in whatever clothes he wore, made him downright lethal. He had to be the most beautiful man she'd ever met. On the beach he had been wearing a pair of jeans and a white shirt. And like her, he had removed his shoes. The outfit would have been casual on any other man but not on him.

Evidently he was single. At least he hadn't had a

ring on his finger, but that meant nothing since her father had rarely worn his wedding ring, either. She wondered if Brandon had someone special living in the States. A businessman traveling alone often forgot certain details like that. As owner of the hotel she was observant and perceptive and knew such affairs were going on under her roof, but as long as they were of mutual consent it was no business of hers.

Cassie reached for the matching shawl to her dress and placed it around her shoulders. The air tonight was rather breezy. Forecasters had reported a tropical storm was stirring up in the Atlantic. Hopefully, it wouldn't become a hurricane, and if it did she hoped that it would not set its course toward the islands.

She glanced at her watch. It was time to meet the very handsome Brandon Jarrett.

Brandon stood near the flower garden, his body shadowed by numerous plants and an abundance of palm trees. He watched Cassie as she left her suite and strolled along the private brick walkway. Like earlier, she hadn't detected his presence and this gave him a chance to study her once again.

The dress she was wearing seemed to have been designed just for her body and was definitely working for her, and for him as well. Just watching her made his pulse rate increase. The lantern lights reflecting off the building highlighted her features. Her hair flowed around her shoulders, tossing around her face with every step she took.

Sensations he hadn't felt in a long time gripped him and they were of a degree he'd never experienced before. John Garrison's youngest daughter was definitely a looker and was having an impact on his senses as well as his body. He inhaled deeply. He had to regain control. He had to remember his plan.

Deciding it wouldn't be in his best interest to catch her off guard for a second time, he deliberately cleared his throat. When she glanced his way their gazes met. He almost forgot everything, except the way she was looking at him. He had never been swept away by a woman, but he felt that he was now standing in sinking sand and quickly decided, just for that moment, he would forget the real reason he was on the island. The woman was too stunningly beautiful for him to do anything else.

"I hope you haven't been waiting long," she said, coming to stand directly in front of him, giving him a close view of her outfit.

"Not at all, but any time I've spent waiting has been worth it," he said, taking her hand in his and feeling the way her hand trembled beneath his fingers. In response, he felt his insides quiver and primitive emotions began stirring in his gut. He was discovering just how strong his sexual attraction to her was.

"Have you decided where we're going?"

Her question invaded his thoughts and he wished he could respond by telling her they were going to find the nearest bed. "Yes, the Viscaya Restaurant. Have you ever heard of it?"

"Yes, I've heard of it," Cassie answered, drawing in a deep breath. "It has an astounding reputation."

"I heard that, as well," he said, holding firm to her hand as he led her through the gardens and toward the parking lot where his rental car was parked. It was a beautiful October night and the breeze off the ocean made it somewhat cool.

"You look nice," Brandon said, opening the door to the Lexus.

She glanced up at him and smiled as she slid onto the car seat. "Thanks. You look nice yourself."

He smiled back at her. "Now it's my time to thank you."

"And you are welcome."

Cassie watched as Brandon crossed in front of the car to get into the driver's side. He did look nice in his dark trousers and crisp white shirt and looked the epitome of sexy. Everything about him appealed to her female senses. His walk was smooth and self-assured.

Before starting the engine he glanced over at her. "The lady at the front desk said the restaurant is only a five-minute drive from here."

Cassie nodded. "All right."

He pulled out of the parking lot and she leaned back into her seat, her body relaxed. She was looking forward to this evening; especially his company. There was a lot she wanted to know about him and decided that now was the time to ask. "So where are you from?"

"I'm from Orlando, Florida," he answered.

"Disney World."

He chuckled. "Yes, Disney World. Have you ever been there?"

"Yes, when I was about ten my mom took me there. We were there for a whole week."

"What about your father?"

A small smile touched her lips. "Dad traveled a lot

and joined us later, but for only a few days." And then, as if she wanted to know more about him, she asked, "And what sort of work you do?"

"I'm an investment broker. My motto is 'If you have any monies to invest then entrust them with me and I'll do the rest.'"

"Umm, that's clever. I like it."

"Thanks. And where are you from, Cassie, and what do you do?" he asked.

Brandon had come to a traffic light and he glanced over at her and saw her nervously rubbing her palms against the side of her dress. Her actions caused him to look at her thighs, the portion her minidress wasn't covering. It took everything within him to force his eyes back on the road when the light changed.

"I was born here on the island and I'm in the hotel business," he heard her say.

Deciding not to put her on the spot by asking her to expound more regarding her occupation he said, "The Bahamas is a beautiful island."

He could tell she had relaxed by the sound of her breathing. "Yes, it is. I take it that this is not your first visit here."

He smiled, liking the sound of her sexy accent. "No, I've been to the island several times, but this is the first time I've stayed at the Garrison Grand-Bahamas."

He didn't think it would be appropriate to mention that he had flown here last year with Jamie in his private plane. It had been then that he had asked her to marry him. She had accepted and they had spent the rest of the week on a yacht belonging to one of his clients, who was also a good friend.

He was grateful when they pulled into the parking lot of the Viscaya Restaurant. For a little while he was getting a reprieve from having to weave more lies.

Less than an hour later Cassie had determined a number of things about Brandon. In addition to being breathtakingly handsome, he was also incredibly charming and outrageously smooth. She'd discovered during dinner that he was also someone who was easy to talk to; someone who had the ability to make her feel comfortable around him. And she noticed he had a tendency to treat all people—from the restaurant's manager to the waiter to the busboy who'd come to clear off their table—with respect. He had made each individual feel important and appreciated.

"That was kind and thoughtful of you," she said when they were walking out of the restaurant.

He glanced over at her. "What?"

"The way you treated everyone back there. You didn't hesitate to let them know how much you appreciated their services. You would be surprised at how many people don't do that," she said, thinking how rudely her hotel workers were often treated by people who thought they were better than them.

He shrugged. "It's something I got from my father. He believed it wouldn't take much for a person to let others know when they've done something right, especially when we are quick to let them know when they've done something wrong."

"It sounds like your father is a very smart man."

"He *was* a smart man. Dad passed away a few years ago," he said.

She glanced over at him and a look of sorrow touched her features. "I'm sorry. Were you close to your father?"

"Yes, we were extremely close. In fact we were partners at our firm," he said truthfully. "My mother died of cancer before I reached my teens so it had been just my dad and I for a long time."

She nodded and then said, "My father passed away a little over four months ago and my mom a month before that."

Brandon heard the pain of her words in her voice and from the light from the electrical torches that lit the parking lot, he actually saw tears in her eyes. He stopped walking just a few feet from where their car was parked and instinctively pulled her into his arms. She offered no resistance when he gathered the warmth of her body against his. He briefly closed his eyes, regretting this cruel game he was playing with her.

"I'm sorry," he whispered in her ear, in a way for both her loss as well as his lies. Her loss was sincere and he actually felt her pain. She had loved both her parents immensely. For the first time since John's death, Cassie Sinclair-Garrison had become a real person and just not a name on a document on a file in his office. And not just the person with whom Parker had a beef.

"I didn't mean to come apart like that," Cassie said, moments later, stepping back out of Brandon's arms, looking somewhat embarrassed.

"It's okay. I can understand the depth of your pain. I've lost both of my parents, but when my mom died at least I had my dad to keep things going, providing a sense of stability in my life. But your parents died fairly close to each other. I can't imagine how you endured such a thing. Do you have other siblings?" he asked, wondering if she would acknowledge the Miami Garrisons.

She gave him a distracted look, as if thinking deeply on his question. Then she said, "My father had other children but I've never met them."

"Not even at the funeral?" he asked, already knowing the answer.

She shrugged. "No, not even then." Then she quickly said, "I'd rather not talk about it anymore, Brandon. It's rather private."

He nodded. "I understand. Sorry for prying."

She reached out and took his hand. "You weren't prying. Everything's sort of complicated right now."

"Again I understand, but if you ever need to talk or need—"

"A shoulder to cry on again," she said, trying to sound cheerful.

He chuckled. "Yes, a shoulder to cry on. I am available."

"Thank you. How long will you be staying at the hotel?"

He paused to open the car door for her. "A week. What about you?"

She waited until she was inside and glanced up at him and said. "Indefinitely. I work at the hotel and depending on how my days are, I sometimes spend the night there instead of driving all the way home. I have a private suite. My home is on the other side of the island."

"I see," Brandon said before closing the door. He

had given her another opportunity but she had yet to tell him she owned the hotel.

After walking around the car and getting inside he turned to her before starting the ignition. "I'm glad you came to dinner with me tonight. What are your plans for tomorrow?"

She smiled. "I have a meeting in the morning and then I'll be leaving for my home. I won't be returning to the hotel until Thursday morning."

Brandon leaned forward and smiled. "Is there anyway I can weasel another dinner date out of you?"

Cassie laughed. "Another dinner date?"

"Yes, I'll even be happy if you wanted to treat me to some of your good cooking."

"And what makes you think I can cook?"

"A hunch. Am I wrong?"

She shook her head. "No, you're right. Not to sound too boastful or conceited, although I don't spend a whole lot of time in the kitchen since I usually eat at the hotel, I can cook. That was one of my mom's biggest rules. And because of it, I was probably one of the few girls in my dorm at college who could fend for herself."

He chuckled. "And where did you attend college?"

"I went to a school in London and got a degree in business administration."

Brandon was still smiling when he finally decided to dig deeper by asking, "And just what is your position at the hotel? You never did say."

From her expression he could tell she was somewhat startled by his question. He was forcing her to make a decision as to whether or not she trusted him enough to tell him that much about herself.

"Evidently," she finally said, "you didn't make the connection when I gave my name earlier tonight."

He lifted a dark brow. "And what connection is that?"

Cassie held on to his gaze. "Garrison. I own the Garrison Grand-Bahamas."

# Three

"You own the hotel?" Brandon asked, seemingly surprised by what she'd said and trying not to place much emphasis on what she'd just revealed and raise her suspicions about his motives for being there.

"Yes, my father left it to me when he died."

Brandon brought the car to a stop at a traffic light and used that opportunity to look directly at her. "Then you must feel proud that he had such faith and confidence in your abilities to do such a thing."

The smile she gave him extended straight from her eyes and he suddenly felt his gut clench from the effect those dark eyes had on him. "Thanks. And he did know of my capabilities because I'd managed the hotel for the past five years."

He nodded when the car began moving again. "That

might be true but I'm sure managing a hotel is a lot different than owning it. It's a big responsibility to place on anyone's shoulders and evidently he felt, and I'm sure justly so, that you could handle the job."

"Thank you for saying that," she said softly. "That was very kind of you."

"I'm just telling you the way I see it," he said, bringing the car to a stop in the parking lot of the hotel. "Now getting back to the subject of seeing you again tomorrow..." he said smoothly.

She shook her head, grinning. "You don't give up, do you?"

"Not without a fight," he said sincerely. "And if you don't feel like having me try out your cooking skills, I'd love to take you to another restaurant tomorrow evening. I understand several in this area come highly recommended."

Trying to ignore the urge to laugh from the intensity of his plea, she smiled. Since she'd taken ownership of her mother's home a few months ago, no man had crossed its threshold and she hadn't planned for one to cross over it anytime soon. But for some reason the thought of Brandon visiting her home didn't bother her, which could only mean one thing. She really liked him.

Pushing her hair away from her face she said, "I would love having dinner again with you tomorrow and I insist it be my treat. At my home. And I will proudly show you just what a good cook I am."

Brandon grinned. "I'll look forward to it."

He got out of the car and walked around it to open the door for her. What he'd said was true. He was looking forward to it but not for the reason that he should be. A part of him wished like hell that her last name wasn't Garrison.

"Thank you, Brandon," she said when he offered her his hand. "I'll leave a sealed envelope with directions to my home for you at the front desk tomorrow," she added when they stood at her door. "It's in Lyford Cay."

"And is there a particular time you prefer that I show up?"

She tilted her head back to look up at him. "Anytime after four will be fine. I won't be serving dinner until around six but I think you might enjoy taking a walk through the aquarium."

He lifted a brow. "The aquarium?"

She smiled. "Yes, my mother loved sea life and ten years ago for her fortieth birthday my father had a beautiful indoor aquarium built for her."

"You live in your mother's home?" he asked when she had lowered her head to get the door key out of her purse.

She glanced back up at him. "It used to be Mom's, but Dad signed it over to me when she died. I really had thought he was going to sell it, but I think the thought of parting with it bothered him since the place held so many special memories."

Brandon didn't know what to say to that. He did know there was no mention of John Garrison owning a home in the Bahamas in any of the legal papers he had. It was a moot point now since, according to Cassie, John had signed it over to her.

"I enjoyed your company tonight," she said, unlocking her door.

Cassie's words drew back his attention. "And I, yours. I'm looking forward to tomorrow."

"So am I. Good night, Brandon."

Although they had just met tonight, he had no intentions of letting her escape inside her suite without them sharing a kiss. All night he had focused on her lips, wondering how they would taste and how they would feel beneath his. He could feel the sizzling tension between them and took a step closer to her, deciding to draw it out and pull it in. He was powerless to do anything less.

He reached out, cupped her chin gently in his hand and studied the dimple she had there. "Nice place for a dimple," he said in a husky voice.

She smiled up at him. "My dad said it's a cleft. He had one, too."

So do his other five children, Brandon thought. "I'm going to have to disagree with your father on that. I have it on good authority that on a man it's a cleft but on a woman it's a dimple."

"Nothing wrong with disagreeing," Cassie said.

His hand felt warm and when he moved it from her chin and took the backside of his hand and caressed the side of her face, she felt her entire body tingle from sensations that not only flooded her mind but also her senses. Without any self-control she released a deep sigh and closed her eyes, thinking his touch felt so soothing. And before she could reopen her eyes she detected the warmth of his lips close to hers, and then she felt it when he placed them softly against her own.

She released another sigh and her lips parted, giving his tongue the opportunity to slip inside and capture hers. She had thought of tasting him all night and she was getting more than she had bargained for. His taste was manly, sexy, delicious—everything she had imagined it would be and more. She couldn't stop the quiver that passed through her body or the moan she heard from low in her throat. He was a master at his game, definitely an expert at what he was doing and how he was making her feel.

Her fingers gripped the sleeve of his shirt when she felt weak in the knees, and in response his arms wrapped themselves around her waist, pulling her closer to him. And she could actually feel his heat, his strength, everything about him that was masculine. Moments later when he broke off the kiss, she opened her eyes.

"Thank you for that," he whispered hoarsely, just inches from her lips. And before she could draw her next breath, he was kissing her again and the pleasure of it was seeping deep into her bones. Instinctively she responded, feeling slightly dizzy while doing so, and she could hear the *purr* that came from deep within her throat.

Moments later he ended the kiss and she regretted the loss, the feel of his mouth on hers. Her gaze latched onto his lips and she felt a warm sensation flow between her legs. Without much effort, he had aroused impulses within her that she had never encountered before. It was like her feminine liberation was threatening to erupt.

"I'm looking forward to seeing you tomorrow, Cassie," he said, taking a step even closer.

The light that shone in her doorway cast the solid planes of his face into sharp focus. She watched as his gaze moved slowly over her features before returning to her eyes. And while his eyes held hers, she studied the deep look of desire in them. For some reason the look didn't startle her, nor did it bother her. What it did do was fill her with anticipation of seeing him again.

"And I'm looking forward to seeing you, as well." When she realized she was still clutching his sleeve she quickly released it, turned and, without wasting time, opened the door and went inside.

A few moments later Brandon entered his own suite as he took a mental note of what had transpired that night. Frankly, he wasn't sure what to make of it. Cassie Garrison was definitely not what he had anticipated. He had expected a woman who was selfish, spoiled, inconsiderate and self-centered. Definitely temperamental at best. However, the woman he had spent time with tonight, in addition to her physical perfection, had possessed charm, style and grace, warmth and sensuality, even while not knowing she was eluding the latter. Then there was her keen sense of intelligence, which was definitely obvious. She was not a woman who acted irrational or who didn't think through any decision she made. Even when she had ordered dinner she had expounded on the advantages of eating healthy. And when she had spoken of her parents he could feel the pain that she'd endured in losing them, pain she was still mending from.

He shook his head, remembering how comfortable she had gotten with him. Surprisingly, they had discovered over the course of their conversation that they had a lot in common. They enjoyed reading the same types of books, shared a dislike of broccoli and had the same taste in music. And when she had opened up to him and revealed she had owned the hotel, he had seen the trusting look in her eyes.

A part of him wished the circumstances were different, that she hadn't lost her parents; that the two of them had met before John's death. And more than anything a part of him wished that he wasn't here betraying her.

In truth, he didn't want to think about that part— he really didn't want to think about Cassie Garrison at all. If only he could let it sink into his mind, as well as his body, that his only reason for being here was purely business and not personal. He of all people knew how it felt to be betrayed. How it felt to have your trust in someone destroyed. And that was not a comforting thought.

He walked out on the balcony and took a moment to stare out at the ocean, hoping he could stop Cassie from whirling through his thoughts. It was a beautiful night, but instead of appreciating the moon and the stars, his mind was getting clouded again with thoughts of a pair of long, gorgeous legs, a mass of curly brown hair cascading around a strikingly beautiful face and the taste of a mouth that wouldn't go away. Kissing her, devouring her lips, had been better than any dessert he'd ever eaten.

Closing his eyes, he breathed in the scent of the ocean, trying to get his mind back in check. That wasn't easy when instead of the ocean's scent filtering through his nostrils it was the scent of Cassie's perfume that wouldn't leave him.

A feeling of uneasiness crept over Brandon. He definitely didn't need this. He was not a man known to get wimpy and all emotional over a woman. Okay, so he had enjoyed her company, but under no circumstances could he forget just who she was and why he was here.

With that thought embedded into his mind and back where it belonged and where he intended for it to stay, he turned and went into his suite.

Craning her neck, Cassie stood at the floor-to-ceiling window in her living room and looked out, watching Brandon's car as it came through the wrought-iron gates that protected her estate.

As the vehicle made its way down the long winding driveway she forced back the shivers that tried overtaking her body when she remembered the night before—every single thing about it. For the first time in a long time she had spent an evening very much aware of a man. No only had she been aware of him, she had actually lusted after him in a way she had never done with a male before. But somehow she had managed to maintain her sensibility and control—at least she had until he had kissed her. And it had been some kiss. Even now those same shivers she tried forcing away earlier were back.

A part of her mind relayed a message to move away from the window when Brandon's car got closer, or else he would see her and assume she was anxiously waiting for him. She lifted her chin in defiance when another part of her sent a different message. Let him think what he wants since she *was* anxiously waiting.

He brought his car to a stop in front of her house and from where she stood she had a very good view of him; one he wouldn't have of her until he got out of the car and halfway up her walkway. She studied his features through the car window and in the light of day he was even more handsome. And when he got out of the car he was dressed as immaculately as he had been the night before.

Today he was wearing a pair of khaki trousers and a chocolate-brown polo shirt. The man was built. He exuded so much sensuality she could actually feel it through the window pane.

She watched him walk away from his car toward her door and suddenly, as if he somehow sensed her, he looked toward the window. His eyes held hers for a moment and then he lifted his hand in a wave, acknowledging her presence.

The heat she had felt earlier in her body intensified and the shivers she couldn't fight slithered through her once more. She lifted her hand to wave back, wondering what it was about him that affected her so. What was there about this man that had her inviting him to her home, her private sanctuary, her personal domain, the place where she felt the presence of her parents the most? Why was she sharing all of that with him?

She discovered she didn't have time to ponder those questions when he disconnected his eyes from hers and headed toward her door. She sighed deeply, her nerves stretched tight. The air she took into her lungs was sharp, and the quickening she felt in her veins was absolute.

Not waiting for a knock at her door, she moved away from the window and headed in that direction, very much aware of the magnetism, the attraction and the lure of the man who was now standing on her doorstep.

* * *

"Welcome to my home, Brandon."

Brandon gazed at Cassie, telling himself that just like last night, his reaction to her was strictly sexual, which accounted for the ache he suddenly felt below the belt. The effect did not surprise him. He accepted it although he didn't like it.

He immediately picked up her scent, the same one that had tortured him through most of the night as if it had been deeply drenched into his nostrils. Reaching out, he took her hand in his, leaned closer and placed a light kiss on the dimple in her chin and finally said, "Thank you for inviting me, Cassie."

He released her hand and she smiled before taking a step back, letting him inside her home. The moment he crossed the threshold he beheld the stunning splendor of the décor. It wasn't just the style and colors, there were also the shapes and designs that combined traditional flare with that of contemporary, colonial and Queen Anne. The mixture in any other place would look crammed, definitely busy. But in this monstrosity of a house it demonstrated a sense of wealth combined with warmth. It also displayed diversity in taste with an unmistakable look of sophistication.

"You have a beautiful home."

Her smile widened. "Thank you. Come let me give you a tour. I haven't changed much since Mom died because she and I had similar taste."

She led and he followed. "Do you take care of this place by yourself?" he asked, although he couldn't imagine one person doing so.

She shook her head. "No, I have a housekeeping

staff, the same one Mom had when she and Dad were alive. My staff is loyal and dedicated and," she said grinning, "a little overprotective where I'm concerned since they've been around since I was twelve."

They came to a spacious room and stopped. He glanced around, appreciating how the entire width of the living room had floor-to-ceiling windows to take advantage of the view of the ocean. He also liked the Persian rugs on the floor.

Beyond the living room was the dining room and kitchen, set at an angle that also took advantage of the ocean's view. The first thing he thought when they walked into the kitchen was that that she had been busy. Several mouthwatering aromas surged through his nostrils and he successfully fought back the grumbling that threatened his stomach.

Both the dining room and kitchen opened to a beautiful courtyard with a stunning swimming pool and a flower garden whose design spread from one area of the yard to the other. Then there was the huge water fountain that sprouted water to a height that seemed to reach the roof.

"Did you live here with your mother?" he asked, moving his gaze over her, taking in the outfit she had chosen to wear today, tropical print tea-length skirt and matching peasant blouse that was as distinctly feminine as she was. The way the skirt flowed over her curves only heightened his sexual desire and made him aware, and very much so, just how much he wanted her.

"Until I left for college," she said, leading him up the stairs. "When I returned from London I got an apartment, but a year later for my birthday Dad bought me a condo. When he gave me the deed to this place, I moved back."

Moments later after giving him a tour of the upstairs, she said with excitement in her voice, "Now I must show you the aquarium."

Once they returned downstairs and rounded corners he saw other rooms—huge rooms for entertaining, a library, a study and room that appeared lined with priceless artwork. He suddenly stopped when he came to a huge portrait hanging on the wall. The man in the painting he recognized immediately, but the woman…

"Your parents?" he asked, staring at the portrait.

"Yes, those are my parents," he heard Cassie say proudly.

Brandon's gaze remained on the woman in the portrait. "She's beautiful," he said. He was so taken by the woman's exquisiteness that he took a step closer to the painting. Cassie followed and glanced over at his fixed look and smiled.

"Yes, Mom was beautiful."

When Cassie began walking away, he strolled beside her, noticing several other photographs of her parents together and some included her. In every one of them John was smiling in a way Brandon had never seen before. To say the man had found true happiness with Ava would be an understatement. The image portrayed on each picture was of a couple who was very much in love, and the ones that included Cassie indicated just how much they loved their daughter, as well.

When they approached another room she stood back to let him enter. His breath literally caught in his throat. On both sides of the narrow but lengthy room were high mahogany cabinets that encased floor-to-ceiling aquariums, each one designed to hide the aquarium frames and waterlines, they were filled with an abundance of tropical and coldwater sea life, seemingly behind a glass wall.

"So what do you think?"

The sound of her voice seemed subdued, but it had a sexy tone just the same. He turned to her. "I think your mother was a very lucky woman to have your father care so deeply to do this for her."

Cassie chuckled. "Oh, Dad knew what would make Mom happy. She had a degree in marine biology and for years worked as a marine biologist at the largest mineral management company on the island."

"Your mother worked?" he asked before he could stop himself.

Cassie didn't seem surprised by his question. "Yes, Mom worked although Dad tried convincing her not to. She enjoyed what she did and she refused to be a kept woman."

At his raised brow, she explained. "My parents never married. He was already married when they met. However they stayed together for over twenty-eight years."

Surprised she had shared that, he asked, "And he never got a divorce from his wife?"

"No. I think at one time he intended to do so when their children got older, but by then things were too complicated."

"Your mother never pushed for a divorce?"

Cassie shook her head. "No. She was comfortable with her place in my father's life as well as his love for her. She didn't need a wedding band or a marriage certificate."

He nodded slowly and deliberately met her gaze when he asked. "What about you? Will you need a wedding band or marriage certificate from a man?"

She grinned. "No, nor do I want one, either. I'm married to the hotel."

"And what about companionship?" he murmured softly, his head tilting to one side as he gazed intently at her. "And what about the idea and thought of a man being here for you? A person who will be there for you to snuggle up to at night. Someone with whom you can get intimate with?"

If the intent of his latter questions were meant to arouse her, it was definitely working, Cassie thought, when a vivid picture flashed through her mind of the two of them sharing a bed, snuggling, making love. Shivers slid down her body and the passion she saw in his eyes was incredibly seductive, too tempting for her well-being.

Trying to maintain her composure with as much effort as she could, she said, "Those happen to be ideas or thoughts that don't cross my mind."

He lifted a dark brow. "They don't?"

"No."

"Umm, what a shame."

"I don't think so. Now please excuse me a moment. I need to check on dinner."

She turned and swiftly left the aquarium.

The moment Cassie rounded the corner to her kitchen she paused and leaned against a counter and inhaled deeply. She had quickly left Brandon because her self-confidence would have gotten badly shaken had she stayed.

He had asked questions she'd only recently thought about herself, but only since meeting him. Last night she had gotten her first experience of a real kiss. She had been filled with the intensity of desire and had never felt such passion. And for the first time in her life she had longed for male companionship, someone to snuggle up close to at night. Someone with whom she could make love. The very thought sent heated shivers down her spine.

Grabbing the apron off a nearby rack and tying it around her waist, Cassie moved away from the counter and went to the sink to wash her hands. She then walked over to the stove where she had a pot simmering…the same way she was simmering inside. It was a low heat that if she wasn't careful, could escalate into a full-fledged flame. And truthfully, she wasn't ready for that.

# Four

Following the smell of a delicious aroma, Brandon tracked his way to the kitchen and suddenly paused. He had seen a lot of feminine beauty in his day, but Cassie Garrison took the cake. Even wearing an apron while standing at a stove stirring a pot, she looked stunning.

She was wearing her hair up but a few errant curls had escaped bondage and were hanging about her ears. Because of her peasant blouse, the top portion of her shoulders was bare and a part of him wanted to cross the room and kiss her, then take his lips and move downward toward her throat and place butterfly kisses along her shoulder blades.

"Something smells good," he said, deciding to finally speak up to remove such lusty thoughts from his mind.

She turned and smiled and not for the first time he

thought she had a pretty pair of lips, ones that had felt well-defined beneath his.

"I hope you're hungry."

He chuckled. "I am. I missed lunch today."

She lifted a brow. "And how did that happen when our brunch buffet is to die for?"

It wouldn't do to tell her that he had missed lunch because he had gotten a call from one of the Miami Garrisons, namely her brother Stephen. "I can believe that. In the two days I've been here I've found your hotel staff to be very efficient at everything they do. The reason I missed out on what I'm sure was such a very delicious meal was I got a call from the office on a few things I needed to finalize."

"Don't they know you're on vacation? My father's rule was to tell the office to hold the calls when you're taking a much-needed break from work, unless it was an extreme emergency."

"Sounds like your father was a smart man."

"He was," Cassie said proudly as her lips formed into another smile. "You would have liked him."

I did, Brandon quickly thought. He leaned against one of the many counters in the kitchen and asked. "So what are you cooking?"

"A number of dishes for you to enjoy. Right now I'm stirring the conch chowder. I've also prepared crab and rice, baked macaroni and cheese and potato salad. For dessert I decided to give you a taste of my grandmother's famous recipe of guava duff."

Brandon felt his lips curve, thinking he wouldn't mind having a taste of her, too. That thought instantly sent his pulse thumping wildly. "Anything I can do to help?" he asked, thinking the best thing to do to keep his mind from wandering was to get busy.

"Let me see…" She said glancing around the room. "I've already washed everything if you want to put the salad together in a bowl."

Relief swept through him, glad she had found him something to do. If he were to continue to stand there and look at her while having all kinds of sexual thoughts, he couldn't be held responsible for his actions.

"Considering my skills in the kitchen, doing what you asked should be reasonably safe," he said, moving toward the sink to wash his hands.

Moments later he was standing at the counter putting the lettuce, tomatoes, cucumbers and onions in a huge bowl for their tossed salad. Knowing he needed to use all the time he had to get to know her, or to find out everything he could about her, he asked, "So, why are you still single, Cassie?"

"Why are you?"

Brandon could tell by her tone that he had once again put her on the defensive. To counter the effect he decided to be honest with her. "Up to a year ago I was engaged to get married."

She stopped stirring the pot and slanted him an arch glance. "If you don't mind me asking, what happened?"

He did mind her asking, but since he initiated the discussion, he would provide her an answer. "My fiancée decided a few months before the wedding that I wasn't everything she needed. I discovered she was unfaithful."

He watched her expression. First surprise and then regret shone in her eyes. "I'm sorry."

"Yes, so was I at the time, but I'm glad I found out before the wedding instead of afterward." Not wanting to discuss Jamie any further, he said, "Salad's done."

She turned back to the stove. "So is everything else. Now we can eat."


Brandon leaned back in his chair after glancing at his plate. It was clean. Cassie hadn't joked when she'd said she knew her way around a kitchen. Everything, even the yeast rolls that had been so fluffy they almost melted in his mouth, had been totally delicious.

He glanced across the table at her. She was finishing the last of the dessert, something that had also been delectable. "The food was simply amazing, Cassie. Thanks for inviting me to dinner."

"You're welcome and I'm glad you enjoyed everything."

"You never did answer the question I asked earlier, about why you're still single. Was I out of line in asking?" he asked, studying the contents of his glass before glancing back at her.

She met his gaze. "No, but there's not a lot to explain. After high school I left home for London to attend college there. I spent my time studying, more so than dating. I didn't see going to college as a way to escape from my parents and start proclaiming my freedom by exerting all kind of outlandish behavior."

"You mean you didn't go to any naked parties? Didn't try any drugs?" He meant the comment as a joke and he could tell she had taken it that way by the smile he saw in her eyes.

"No, there were no naked parties, no drugs and no

eating of fried worms just to fit in with any group." She grinned and added, "I mostly hung alone and I lived off campus in an apartment. Dad insisted. And the only reason he agreed that I have a roommate was for safety reasons."

"So you never dated during college?"

"I didn't say that," she said, taking a sip of her wine. "I dated some but I was very selective when I did so. Most of the guys at college enjoyed a very active sex life and didn't mind spreading that fact or the names of the girls who helped them to reach that status. I didn't intend to be one of them. I had more respect for myself than that."

Brandon stared down at his wine, considering all she had said. He then looked back up at her. "Are you saying you've never been seriously involved with anyone?"

She smiled warmly. "No, that's not what I'm saying." She paused for a moment before adding softly, "There was someone, a guy I met after college. Jason and I dated and thought things were working out but later discovered they weren't."

"What went wrong?"

The memory of that time filled Cassie's mind and for some reason she didn't have a problem sharing it with him. "He began changing in a way that wasn't acceptable to me. He would break our dates and make dumb excuses for doing so. And then out of the clear blue sky one day he broke off with me, and it was then that he told me the reason why. He had taken up with an older woman, a wealthy woman who wanted him as a boy toy, and he felt that was worth kicking aside what I thought we had."

Brandon stared at her. "How long ago was that?"

"Almost four years ago."

"Have you seen him at all since that time?" he asked.

She took another sip of her wine and suddenly felt quite warm. "Of course we haven't dated since then, but yes, I've seen him. He was thoughtful enough to attend my mother's funeral."

And then Cassie said, "And when I saw him I knew that our breakup was the best thing and I owed him thanks. That was a comforting thought and I no longer could hate him."

Brandon stared down into his wine, absently twirling the glass between his fingers, wondering if she ever discovered the truth about him—who he was and why he was there—would she end up hating him, too.

"You've gotten quiet on me," she said.

He glanced back up at her, held her gaze and then reached across the table and took her hand in his. "Have I? If so, it's because I can't imagine any man letting you go," he said softly, tightening his hold on her hand.

A shiver ran down Cassie's spine. She felt the sincerity in Brandon's words and they touched her. She stared at him, totally aware of his physical presence, and with his hand holding hers she felt his strength. Warmth flooded her from the heat she saw in his eyes and for a tiny moment a wealth of meaning shone in them.

"And while you were telling me about your ex-fiancée," she said, her eyes holding steady on his face, "I couldn't help thinking the same thing. I can't imagine any woman letting you go, either."

It seemed the room suddenly got quiet. The only sounds were that of their breathing in a seemingly strained and forced tone. And he was still holding her hands and she felt his fingers move as they brushed across her hand in soft, featherlike strokes. The beating of her heart increased and his gaze continued to hold hers. The expression on his face was unreadable but the look in his eyes was not.

He slowly stood and pulled her out of her seat. Wordlessly, he brought her closer to him. Heat was thrumming through her and she drew in a slow breath. She slid her gaze from his eyes and lowered them to his lips. He leaned in closer, inching his mouth closer to hers.

Cassie felt the heat within her intensify just seconds before he brushed his lips across hers, causing a colossal sensation that she felt all the way to her toes, before spreading to areas known and unknown. And when a sigh of pleasure escaped her lips, easing them apart, with a ravenous yet gentle entry he began devouring her mouth.

Brandon felt the rush of blood that started in his head, and when it got to his chest it joined the rapid pounding of his heart. This was what energized passion was all about. And as he deepened the kiss all kind of feelings reverberated through him, searing awareness in his central nervous system. When he took hold of her tongue, he was filled with intense yearning and a craving that for him was unnatural.

He slightly shifted his stance and brought her closer to the fit of him, and to a body that was getting aroused by the minute. By the moans he heard coming from her he could tell she was enjoying the invasion of his tongue. That realization had him sinking deeper and deeper into the taste and texture of her mouth.

Her body pressed against his hard erection, making him want to sweep her into his arms and carry her to the nearest bedroom. He knew it would be sheer madness. And it would also be wrong. She deserved more than a man making love to her for all the wrong reasons, a man who had walked into her life without good intensions. A man who was even now betraying her.

That thought had him ending the kiss but he couldn't let her go just yet, so he pulled her closer into his arms. How had he allowed himself to get into this situation? How had he let Cassie get to him so quickly and so deeply?

She pulled slightly back, glanced out the window and then back at him and smiled. "Do you want to take a stroll on the beach before it gets too dark?"

"I'd love to," he said, releasing her.

"It will only take a minute for me to get my shawl. You can wait for me on the terrace if you'd like."

"All right."

She shifted to move past him and he suddenly reached out and gently locked his hand on her arm. Then he raised his hands to her hair and brushed back the strands that had fallen in her face. He felt the shiver that touched her body the moment he leaned down and brushed a kiss against her lips. "I'll be waiting," he whispered.

A few moments later Cassie quietly slipped out on the terrace to find Brandon standing with his back to her, staring out at the ocean with both hands in the pockets of his trousers.

His stance radiated so much sex appeal it should

have been illegal. He seemed to be in deep thought and she couldn't help wondering what he was thinking about. Had talking about his ex-fiancée opened up old wounds? Having someone you loved betray you wasn't easy to take. She had discovered that with Jason.

"I'm ready."

He turned at the sound of her voice and across the brick pavers she met his gaze. He then looked at her from head to toe, zeroing in on her bare feet for a few seconds.

She laughed. "Hey, don't look surprised. You never walk on the beach with shoes on. That's an islander rule, so please remove yours."

He chuckled as he dropped into a wicker chair to take off his shoes and socks. She thought the feet he exposed were as sexy as the rest of him. Placing his socks and shoes aside, he stood and smiled at her. "Happy now?"

"Yes, extremely. Now we can make footprints in the sand." She held her hand out to him. "Let's go."

Brandon took the hand she offered and together they walked down the steps toward the private beach.

"So, tell me about your life in Orlando."

Her question reminded him of the lies he had planted, as well as those he had to continue to tell. He glanced over at her and asked, "What do you want to know?"

Smiling curiously, she asked, "Is there someone special in your life waiting for your return?"

"No," he responded with no hesitation. "I date occasionally but there's no one special."

Seconds ticked by and when she didn't say anything he decided to add, "And it isn't because I mistrust all women because of what my ex-fiancée did. I got over it and moved on. I buried myself in my work because while with her I spent a lot of time away from it. That's what she wanted and what I thought she needed."

"But you found it wasn't?"

"Yes, I found it wasn't, especially when it wasn't for the right reason. Jamie had an insecurity complex and I fed into it. But that wasn't enough. She had to feel doubly safe by having someone else in her life, besides me."

"Did she not care how that would play out once you discovered the truth?"

He shrugged. "I guess she figured she would never get caught. She even went so far to admit that she would not have given up her lover after we married."

"Sounds like she was pretty brazen."

His jaw tightened. "Yes, she was."

When they reached the end of the shore they stopped and looked out at the ocean. Standing beside her Brandon could feel Cassie's heat, and even with the scent of the sea he inhaled her fragrance. He allowed the rest of his senses to appreciate her presence, being with her at this time and place.

She turned and flashed him a brilliant smile. "The sunset is beautiful, isn't it?"

"Yes, and so are you."

She lowered her head as if to consider his words. She then looked back at him. "Are you always this complimentary with women?"

"No, not always."

"Then I should feel special."

"Only because you are."

She turned and pressed her lithe body against his aroused one, and he was tempted to lower his head and connect to the lips she was so eagerly offering him. Instead he stepped back and said, "I think it's time for me to leave and go back to the hotel now."

He saw the questions in her eyes and really wasn't surprised when she asked, "Why, Brandon?"

He understood her reason for asking. But there was no way he could be completely honest with her. "I don't think we're ready for that step yet," he murmured softly, moving forward to pull her in his arms.

She leaned back and looked at him as her lips curved into a smile. "Are you talking for yourself or for me?"

He ignored the underlying challenge in her words. "I'm trying to be a gentleman and speak for the both of us."

"I'm a grown woman, Brandon. I can speak and think for myself."

He looked down at her, studied her eyes and saw the deep rooted stubbornness glaring in them. "I know that, but I want you to trust me to know what's best for the both of us right now."

She paused then said, "All right, but only on one condition."

He raised a dark brow. "And what condition is that?"

"That we have dinner again tomorrow night."

It was on the tip of Brandon's tongue to tell her that he was thinking seriously about returning to Miami tomorrow. Parker and Stephen would know soon enough that his mission hadn't been accomplished. The thought of spending time with Cassie one more night over dinner was something he couldn't pass up. But then, he would give her an out by suggesting a place she probably wouldn't go along with.

"Dinner will be fine as long as we can dine at the hotel," he said.

He was surprised when she nodded and said, "All right."

Brandon nodded. "Come on, let's go back."

When they reached the terrace he stopped and turned to her. "And I might have to go back to the States on Thursday. Something has come up that needs my attention."

He could see the disappointment in her face and it almost weakened his resolve.

"I understand. I'm a businesswoman, so I know how things can come up when you least expect them to…or want them to."

He eased down in the wicker chair to put back on his shoes and socks. He waited and then said, "I'm looking forward to having dinner with you tomorrow."

"So am I."

He glanced up at her, intrigued by the eagerness in the tone of her voice, and wondered if perhaps she was plotting his downfall. He wanted her with a fierce passion and it wouldn't take much to push him over the edge.

Brandon stood, knowing it was best for him to leave now. Hanging around could result in more damage than good. "Will you walk me to the door?"

He reached for her hand and she didn't resist in giving it to him. When they reached her front door he gazed at her, thinking he wouldn't be forgetting her for a long time. "Thanks again for a beautiful evening and a very delicious dinner."

The smile that appeared on her face was genuine. "You are welcome." And then she leaned up on tiptoes and brushed a kiss across his lips. "I'll see you at dinner tomorrow, Brandon. Please leave a note at the front desk regarding where you want us to meet and when."

Brandon held her gaze for a moment, and then nodded before turning to walk down the walkway to his car.

# Five

Brandon glanced at the table that sat in the middle of the floor. Room service had done an outstanding job of making sure his orders were followed. He wanted Cassie to see the brilliantly set table the moment she arrived.

He had tried contacting Parker earlier today to let him know his trip hadn't revealed anything about Cassie that they didn't already know. He shook his head, thinking that he stood corrected on that. There was a lot about her that he knew now that he hadn't known before, but as far as he was concerned it was all good, definitely nothing that could be used against her.

Parker's secretary had told him that his friend had taken a couple of days off to take his wife Anna to New York for shopping and a Broadway show, and wouldn't be returning until the beginning of next week. Brandon couldn't help but smile every time he thought about how the former Anna Cross had captured the heart of the man who had been one of Miami's most eligible bachelors and most prominent businessman.

He turned at the sound of the knock on the door and quickly crossed the room. As he'd expected, she was on time. He opened the door to find Cassie standing there, and smiled easily. As usual she looked good. Tonight her hair was hanging around her shoulders. He studied her face and could tell she was wearing very little makeup, which was all that was needed since she had such natural beauty.

His gaze slid down her body. She was no longer wearing the business suit he had seen her in earlier that day when he had caught a glimpse of her before she had stepped into an elevator. Instead she had changed into a flowing, slinky animal-print dress that hugged at the hips before streaming down her figure. A matching jacket was thrown over her arm. A pair of black leather boots were on her feet, but how far up her legs they went he couldn't tell due to the tea-length of her dress. He knew she was wearing the boots more for a fashion statement than for the weather.

"May I come in?"

He pulled his gaze back to her face and returned her smile. "Yes, by all means."

Her fragrance filled his nostrils when she strolled by him and after closing the door he stood there and stared at her with his hands shoved in the pockets of his trousers. He had placed them there so he wouldn't be tempted to reach out and pull her into his arms. That temptation was becoming a habit.

"You look nice," he couldn't help but say because she did look nice, so nice that he felt the fingers inside his pockets beginning to tingle.

"Thank you. And you look nice yourself."

When he lifted a skeptical brow he saw her smile widen, and then she said, "You do look nice. I thought that the first time I saw you."

"That night on the beach?"

"No, that day you checked in to the hotel. I happened to notice you and immediately knew by the way you were dressed that you were an American businessman."

He nodded, not wanting to get in to all the other things that he was, especially when his conscience was getting pinched. He decided to change the subject. "I hope you're hungry."

"I am." She glanced around and saw the table. "They've delivered already?"

Freeing his hands from his pockets, he moved away from the door to cross the room to where she stood. "No, they've just set up everything. I didn't want to take the chance of ordering something you didn't like."

He reached for the menu he had placed on the table. "You want to take a look?"

She shook her head. "No, I have every entrée on it memorized."

He chuckled. "I'm impressed."

She grinned. "Just one of my many skills. And if I may…"

"And you can."

"Then I would recommend the Salvador. It's a special dish that's a combination of lobster, fish, crawfish and various other seafood that's stewed and then served over rice."

"Sounds delicious."

"It is, but I have to warn you that it's kind of spicy."

A smile curved his lips. "I can handle a little bit of spicy. And please make yourself comfortable while I phone room service."

Cassie placed her jacket across the back of the sofa and sat, crossing her legs. She hadn't missed the look of male appreciation in Brandon's eyes when he had opened the door. His already dark gaze had gotten darker and his seductive look had sent heat flowing through her body.

Deciding she needed to cool down, she glanced around. The layout of this suite was similar to one she used whenever she stayed overnight at the hotel. However since hers was an executive suite, it was slightly larger and also had a kitchen, although she never used it.

"Our dinner will be delivered in about thirty to forty-five minutes," he said, sitting on the sofa beside her and shifting his position to face her. "So, how was your day?"

She rolled her eyes and shook her head. "Crazy. Hurricane Melissa can't seem to make up her mind which way she wants to go, so we're taking every pre-caution. Just yesterday she was headed north, but now she's in a stall position as if trying to decide if she really wants to go north after all. We had a number of people who decided not to take any chances and have checked out of the hotel already."

Brandon nodded. He'd been keeping up with the

weather reports as well and understood her concern. Being a native of Miami, he had experienced several hurricanes in his lifetime, some more severe than others. Earlier that day he had spoken with his secretary, Rachel Suarez. A Cuban-American, Rachel had been working for his firm for over thirty years, and had started out with his father. When it came to handling things at the office she could hold her own— including the possibility of an oncoming hurricane.

"And if the hurricane comes this way I'm sure your staff knows what to do," he said, tempted to ease over toward her and run his hands up her legs to see how far up her boots went.

"Trust me, they know the drill. Every employee has to take a hurricane awareness course each year. It prepares them for what to do if it ever comes to that. Dad mandated the training after we went through Hurricane Andrew."

Brandon remembered Hurricane Andrew, doubted he would ever be able to forget it. It had left most of Miami, especially the area where he had lived, in shambles. "Well, hopefully Lady Melissa will endure a peaceful death before hitting land," he said mildly.

He then asked, "Would you like anything to drink while we wait? How about a glass of wine?"

"That would be nice. Thanks."

He stood and Cassie watched as he did so. She watched him walk across the room, thinking he was so sinfully handsome it was a shame. His gray trousers and white shirt were immaculate, tailored to fit his body to perfection. Last night he had done the gentlemanly thing and had stopped anything from escalating further between them, and after he had left her home she had felt grateful. Now she felt a sense of impending loss. He would be leaving tomorrow and chances where they would never see each other again.

For the past two days she had felt alive and in high spirits, something she hadn't felt in the last five months—and all because of him. He hadn't pushed for an affair with her. In fact when he'd had a good opportunity to go for a hit, he had walked away. Had he exerted the least bit of pressure, she would have gladly taken him into her bed. There had never been a man who'd had her entertaining the idea of a casual fling before. But Brandon Jarrett had.

"Here you are."

She looked up. Their gazes connected and she reached out to take the wineglass he offered, struggling to keep her fingers from trembling. "Thanks." She immediately took a sip, an unladylike gulp was more like it. She needed it. The heat within her was intensifying.

"You okay?"

She favored him with a pleasing smile. "Yes, I'm fine." She held on to the look in his eyes and then asked, "And are you okay?"

He returned her smile. "Yes."

She lowered her head to take another sip of her drink, trying to ignore the towering figure standing in front of her. She sensed his movement away from her, but refused to lift her head just yet to see where he had gone. Moments later when she did so, she drew in a quick breath. He was standing across the room with a wineglass in his hand, leaning against the desk and staring at her. Not just staring, but he seemed to be stirring up the heat already engulfing her. Then there were pleasure points that seemed to be touching various parts of her body. She was a sensible woman but at the moment she felt insensible, deliriously brazen. She knew what she wanted but inwardly debated being gutsy enough to get it. But then, as awareness flowed between them, she was compelled to do so.

With his eyes still holding hers, she stood and slowly began crossing the room to him. His strength, as well as his heat, was filtering across to her, touching her everywhere, and putting her in a frame of mind to do things she'd never done before. He watched her every step, just as she watched how the darkness of his eyes did nothing to cloak the desire in his gaze. It was desire that she felt in every angle of her body, in every curve and especially in the juncture of her legs. Especially there.

When she reached him she stood directly in front of him, still feeling his strength and heat, and still radiating in desire. With great effort she held on to the wineglass in her hand, needing another sip to calm her nerves, to quench her heat.

She lifted the glass to her lips and after taking a quick sip, Brandon reached out and took the glass from her, leaned in and placed his lips where the glass had been.

Brandon's heart was pounding furiously in his chest and every muscle in his body ached. Fire was spreading through his loins and a quivering sensation was moving through him at a rapid pace. Her mouth had opened beneath his and he tasted her with a ravenous hunger that was gripping him, conquering with a need he could no longer contain.

Pulling back, he placed both of their glasses on the table, and with his hands now free he took her into his arms and quickly went back to kissing her with a passion that was searing through him. With very little effort his mouth coaxed her to participate. Once he took hold of her tongue, he strived to reach his goal of ultimate satisfaction for the both of them.

What they were exchanging was a sensual byplay of tongues that was meant to excite and arouse. Their bodies were pressed so close that he could feel the tips of her breasts rub against his chest. He could feel the front of her cradle his erection in a way that had his heartbeat quickening and his body getting harder. A need to make her his was seeping through every pore. He lowered his hand and pulled her even closer to his aroused frame, as he was in serious danger of becoming completely unraveled.

She pulled back and breathed in deeply, her arms wrapped tightly around his neck. It only took a look into her eyes to see the fire burning in their depths. That look made him feel light-headed. The room seemed to be revolving, making him dizzy with smoldering desire. The experience was both powerful and danger-ous. His lungs released a shuttering breath and a part of him knew he should do what he'd done last night and walk away. But his wants and needs had him glued to the spot.

And then she rose on tiptoe and whispered. "Make love to me, Brandon."

Her words, spoken in a sexy breath, broke whatever control he had left, every single thread of it. With a surge of desire that had settled in his bones, he swept her off her feet and into his arms and headed straight for the bedroom.

Cassie's heart began thumping in her chest when Brandon placed her on the king-size four-poster bed. And when he stood back and gave her that look, like she was a morsel he was ready to devour, she automatically squeezed her legs together to contain the heat flowing between them. There was an intensity, a desperation bursting within her, but not for any man. Just this one.

Since meeting him she hadn't been able to put him out of her mind. Even as crazy as today had been, periodically he had found a way to creep into her thoughts. And she had felt herself getting flushed when she thought about the kisses they had shared. The memories had been unsettling on one hand and then soothing on the other. His kisses had easily aroused her and had made every nerve in her body quiver…like they were doing now.

She watched as he slowly began unbuttoning his shirt before shrugging broad shoulders to remove it. Her gaze zeroed in on his naked chest and suddenly her mind began indulging in fantasies of placing kisses all over it. She held her breath watching, waiting for him to start taking off his pants. However, instead of doing so, he walked back over to the bed.

"Do you know what I want to know? What I have to know?" he asked, staring at her from top to bottom.

Her mind went blank. She didn't have a clue. "What," she murmured, feeling the sexual tension that had overtaken the room.

"I have to know how far up your legs those boots go."

That definitely was not what she had expected him

to say and couldn't help but smile. "Why don't you find out," she challenged silkily.

Brandon took a couple of steps toward the bed, reached out and slowly raised her dress. He sucked in a deep breath as he lifted it higher and higher. The top of the boots ended just below her knee, giving him a tantalizing view of her thighs.

"Satisfied?"

He shifted his gaze from her legs and thighs back to her face. "Partially. But I will be completely satisfied in a moment."

Cassie swallowed when Brandon unzipped her boots and began removing them, taking the time to massage her legs and ankles and the bottom of her feet. "Do you want to know something else?" he asked her.

"What?"

"I stayed awake most of the night just imagining all the things I'd like doing to you if ever given the chance," he said in a husky tone.

"Now you have the chance."

He smiled. "I know." He took a step back. "Scoot over here for a second."

She eased across the bed to him on her knees and he tugged her dress over her head, leaving her clad in a black satin bra and a pair of matching panties. He tossed the dress aside with an expression on his face denoting he was very pleased with what he had done.

Cassie was very pleased with what he had done, too. "Not fair," she said sulkily. "You have on more clothes than I do."

He chuckled. "Not for long." His hands went to the snap on his pants.

Reasonably satisfied with his answer, as well as more than satisfied with what she was seeing, Cassie watched as Brandon begin easing down his zipper, her gaze following every movement of his hand. This wasn't her first time with a man, but it had been a while. And this was the first time one had gotten her so keyed up. What she was seeing was sending shivers rippling down her spine.

She nearly groaned when he stepped out of his pants. The only thing covering his body was a pair of very sexy black briefs—briefs that could barely support his huge erection, but were trying like hell to do so. She stared when he removed them. Then she blinked and stared some more. And in a move that was as daring as anything she had ever done, she scooted to the edge of the bed, reached out and stroked over his stomach with her hand before moving it lower to cup him.

She glanced up when she heard his sharp intake of breath. "Am I hurting you?" she asked softly, as she continued to fondle him in a way she had never done with a man before. Even with Jason she hadn't been this bold.

"No, you're not hurting me but you are torturing me," she heard Brandon say through clenched teeth. "There's a difference."

"Is there?"

"Yes, let me show you." He reached his hands behind her back and undid her bra clasp. He eased off her bra and tossed it aside and his hands immediately went to her naked breasts. And then he began stroking her as precisely and methodically as she was stroking him. A startled gasp erupted from her throat when he took things just a little further and leaned over and caught a nipple between his lips.

Suddenly, she understood the difference between pain and torture. She understood it and she felt it. This was torture of the most exhilarating kind. It was the type that filled you with an all-consuming need, an intense sexual craving. When he switched his mouth to the other breast she released a deep moan, thinking his tongue was wonderfully wicked.

"I can't take much more," she muttered in an abated breath.

"That makes two of us," he said, lifting his head. "But I'm not through with you yet."

He moved to grab his pants off the floor, pulled a condom packet from his wallet and put it on. He then eased her back on the bed and gently grabbed a hold of her hips to remove her panties. She heard the deep-throated growl when she became completely bare to his view. She saw the look in his eyes; felt the intensity of his gaze, and immediately knew where his thoughts were going. He glanced at her, gave her one hungry, predatory smile and before she could draw in her next breath he lifted her hips to his mouth.

Cassie screamed out his name the moment his tongue invaded her and she grabbed on to the bedspread, knowing she had to take a hold of something. He was taking her sensuality to a whole new dimension and shattering her into a million pieces, bringing on the most intense orgasm ever. She continued writhing under the impact of his mouth while sensations tore through her. And while her body was still throbbing, he pulled back and shifted his body in position over hers. Their gazes locked, held, while he eased into her, joining their bodies as one.

Brandon sucked in sharply as he continued to sink deeper and deeper into Cassie's body, fulfilling every fantasy he'd had about her. Securing his hips over hers he then used both hands to lock in her hair as he lowered his head to capture her mouth. He began rocking against her, thrusting into her as she gave herself to him, holding nothing back. He felt her inner muscles clench him, while a whirlwind of emotions washed over the both of them.

"Brandon!"

When he felt her come apart under him, he followed suit and exploded inside of her. He felt heaven. He felt overwhelmed. He felt a degree of sensuality that he knew at that moment could only be shared with her.

Moments later he gathered her closer into his arms, their breathing hard, soft, then hard again. He slowly moved his hand to caress her thigh and stomach, still needing to touch her in some way.

Deep down Brandon knew he should not have made love to her without first telling her the truth of who he was and why he was there. He didn't want to think about how she would react to the news and hopefully, she would hear him out and give him time to explain. More than anything, she deserved his honesty. "Cassie?"

It took her a long time to catch her breath to answer. "Yes?" She lifted slightly and looked at him for a moment before saying, "Please don't tell me that you regret what we shared, Brandon."

He shook his head. Boy, was she way off. "I have no regrets but there's something I need to tell you."

She lifted a brow. "What?"

He opened his mouth to speak at the exact moment there was a knock on the door. A part of him felt temporary relief. "Dinner has arrived. We can talk later."

Like Cassie had said it would be, dinner was delicious. But it would be hard for any man to concentrate on anything when he had a beautiful woman sitting across from him wearing nothing but a bathrobe. And the knowledge that she was stark naked underneath was not helping matters.

He had assumed, when he had slipped back into his shirt and trousers to open the door for room service, that she would put back on her clothes, as well. He had been mildly surprised, but definitely not disappointed, when she had appeared after the food was delivered wearing one of the hotel's complimentary bath robes.

Deciding to take his mind off his dinner guest and just what he would love to do to her…again, he glanced out the French doors and onto the terrace. In the moonlight he could tell that the ocean waves were choppy and by the way the palm trees were swaying back and forth, he knew there was a brisk breeze in the air. Even if Hurricane Melissa decided not to come this way, she was still stirring up fuss.

"Brandon?"

He glanced over at Cassie. She had said his name with a sensual undercurrent, making him get aroused again, especially when he saw the top of her robe was slightly opened, something she'd evidently taken the time to do while he had been looking out the French doors. A smile tugged at his lips. She was trying to tempt him and he had no complaints. In fact, he more than welcomed her efforts. When it came to her he was definitely easy. "Yes?"

"Right before dinner you said you needed to talk to me about something."

He nodded. He had dismissed the thought of discussing anything over dinner. The last thing he'd wanted was the entire meal flung at his head. And in a way he didn't want to talk about anything now since he knew how the evening would end once he did so. But he couldn't overlook the fact that he owed her the truth.

She was giving him a probing look, waiting on his response. He was about to come clean and tell her everything when a cell phone went off. From the sound of the ringer he knew it wasn't his and she jumped up and walked quickly to grab her purse off the sofa and pulled her cell phone out.

"Yes?" After a few moments she said, "All right, Simon. Let me know if anything changes." Cassie held the phone in her hand for a moment before putting it back in her purse.

"Bad news?"

She glanced up and met Brandon's gaze. "Nothing that surprises me. Forecasters predict Hurricane Melissa will escalate to a category three whenever she makes it to shore."

Brandon nodded. "So she's moving again?"

"No, she's still out in the Atlantic gaining strength. Wherever she decides to land is in for a rough time."

And more than anyone Cassie knew what that meant. Because of the uncertainty, more people would be checking out of the hotel. She really didn't blame them and didn't begrudge anyone who put their safety first. But that also meant chances were Brandon would be leaving tomorrow, as well, possibly earlier in the day than he had planned. If Hurricane Melissa turned its sights toward the Bahamas, the airports would be closing, which wouldn't be good news to a lot of people.

Today things at the hotel had been crazy, but she had a feeling tomorrow things would get even crazier. She would probably be too busy to spend any time with Brandon before he left, which meant tonight was all they had. The thought of never seeing him again pricked her heart more than she imagined it would. And she knew what she wanted. She wanted memories that would sustain her after he left. They would be all she would have in the wee hours of the morning when she would want someone to snuggle close to, someone to make love to her the way he had done earlier. Those nights when she would ache from wanting the hard feel of him inside of her, she would have her memories.

He had said that he had something to tell her and a part of her had an idea just what that something was. A disclaimer that stated spending time with her, sharing a bed with her, had been an enjoyable experience, but he had to move on and he wouldn't keep in touch. She couldn't resent him for it because he hadn't made any promises, nor had he offered a commitment. What they were sharing was an island fling and nothing else and chances were he wanted to make sure she understood that.

She did.

And she wouldn't have any regrets when he left. Knowing all of that, she knew what she wanted. More than anything, tonight she wanted to spend the rest of her time making love and not talking.

Deciding not to be denied what she wanted, and knowing his eyes were on her, she untied the sash at her waist to remove her robe and dropped it where she stood. She brazenly moved to cross the room to him stark naked. He stood and began removing his clothes, as well. For the second time that night she felt daring and the look in his eyes while he pulled a condom out of his pocket and put it on over his huge erection, once again made her feel desirable.

They stood in front of each other completely naked and their mouths within inches of each other, emanated intense heat. He leaned down and captured her mouth. Unlike earlier that night, there was nothing gentle about this kiss. It conveyed a hunger that she felt as he plunged deeply and thoroughly in her mouth, at the same time he wrapped her arms tightly around her. His taste was spicy and reminded her of the food they'd eaten for dinner. The flavor of him exploded against her palate when her tongue began tangling with his.

Her body began quivering, all the way to her bones, and she felt heat collect in the area between her legs. Only Brandon could bring her to this state, escalating her need for passion of the most intense kind. She felt the powerful beating of his heart in his chest, sending vibrations through her breasts, tantalizing her nipples and making them throb, the same way she was throbbing in the middle.

She pulled back, hauled in a gasping breath, and before she could recover, he began walking her backward toward the sofa. She was glad when they finally made it there since her knees felt like they would give out at any moment. She sank back against the sofa cushions, and then he was there, his mouth and hands everywhere, and it took all she had not to give into the earth-shaking pleasure and scream.

And then he did the unexpected, he pulled her up with him turning her so her back pressed against his chest. He leaned over and began placing kisses along her throat and neck while his hand moved up and down her stomach before capturing her breasts in his hand. He cupped them, gently squeezed them, teased her sensitive nipples to harden beneath his fingertips.

"Open your legs for me." He murmured the request hotly against her ear while his hands moved from her breasts and traveled lower to the area between her legs. He stroked her while breathing heavily in her ear. Electric currents, something similar to bolts of lightning, slammed through her with his touch. Moments later another orgasm exploded within her but she had a feeling he wasn't through with her yet.

"Lean forward and hold on to the back of the sofa," he said with a raw, intense sexuality in his breath.

As soon as she stretched her arms out and grabbed hold of the sofa, she felt him grind the lower part of his body against her. He took his hands and tilted her hips before easing his shaft into her. He went deep, and she felt him all the way to her womb.

"Brandon!"

He began thrusting back and forth inside of her, sending sensations rippling all through her. Establishing a rhythm that was splintering her apart both inside and out, he grabbed hold of her breasts again and used his fingertips and thumb to drive her over the edge.

She cried out his name when her body exploded and when he plunged deeper inside of her she could feel the exact moment an explosion hit him, as well. She groaned when a searing assault was made on her senses, and when he pulled her head back and took control of her mouth she felt his possession.

Before she could get a handle on that feeling, she felt him scoop her into his arms and carry her into the bedroom.

The ringing phone woke Cassie and, instinctively, she reached over and picked it up. When she heard Brandon's voice engaged in a conversation with someone, she quickly recalled where she was and realized that he had gotten out of the bed earlier to take a shower and had picked up the bathroom's phone.

She was about to hang up when she recognized the voice of the man he was talking to. She immediately sat up straight in bed, knowing she was right when she head Brandon call the man by name. Why would Brandon be talking to Parker Garrison? How did they even know each other? Just what was going on?

Hanging up the phone, she angrily slipped out of bed. Ignoring the soreness in the lower part of her body, she glanced around, looking for her clothes, and hurriedly began putting them on. Her mind was spinning with a thousand questions as she tried getting her anger under control. She had just tugged her dress over her head when she heard Brandon enter the room.

"Good morning, sweetheart."

She swung around after pulling her dress down her body. Trembling with rage, she tried remaining calm as she crossed the room to face Brandon. A part of her didn't want to believe that this man, who had tenderly made love to her last night, who had taken her to the most sensuous heights possible in his arms, could be anything other than what she saw. Utterly beautiful. The epitome of a perfect gentleman, who was thoughtful and kind.

Something in her eyes must have given her away, and when he reached for her hand, she took a step back. "What's wrong, Cassie?" he asked in a voice filled with concern.

Instead of answering his question she had one of her own. Swallowing the lump she felt in her throat and with a back that was ramrod straight, she asked, "How do you know Parker Garrison, Brandon?"

# Six

There was a long silence as Brandon and Cassie stood there, staring at each other. Tension in the room was thick, almost suffocating. Brandon inhaled deeply, wishing like hell that he'd told her the truth last night as he had intended and not have her find out on her own. Apparently, she had listened to his phone conversation long enough to know the caller had been Parker.

"I asked you a question, Brandon. How do you know Parker?"

Her sharp tone cut into his thoughts and he could tell from her expression that she was beginning to form her own opinions about things. He didn't want that. He took another deep breath before saying, "He's a client."

She turned her face from him with the speed of someone who had been slapped and the motion made his heart turn over in his chest. He had hurt her. He could actually feel it. The thought that he had done that to her appalled him and at that moment he felt lower than low. "Cassie, I—"

"No," she snapped, turning back to him.

She reached up as if to smooth a strand of hair back from her face, but he actually saw her quickly swipe back a tear. Brandon winced.

"And just what do you do for Parker, Brandon? Are you his hit man? Since I'm not being cooperative did he decide to do away with me all together?"

"I'm his attorney, Cassie," he asserted, his brows drawing together in a deep frown, not liking what she'd said.

"His attorney?" she whispered, her eyes widening in disbelief.

His stomach tightened when he saw the color drain from her face. "Yes," he said softly. "I represent Garrison, Inc."

She didn't say anything for a few moments but the shocked eyes staring at him appeared as jagged glass. Then they appeared to turn into fire. "Is Brandon Jarrett even your real name?" she blurted.

He exhaled a long breath before answering. "Yes, but not my full name. It's Brandon Jarrett Washington."

Cassie frowned. She recalled seeing the name of Washington and Associates law firm on a letterhead sent to her on Parker's behalf a few months ago when she had refused to acknowledge any more of his phone calls. "I should have known," she said with anger in her voice. "Anything that's too good to be true usually isn't true. So what sort of bonus did Parker offer you to make me change my mind about the buyout? He evidently told you to succeed by using any means necessary. You wasted your time in law school since you would make a pretty good gigolo."

"Don't say that, Cassie."

"Don't say it?" she repeated as intense anger radiated from every part of her. "How dare you tell me not to. You came here pretending to be someone you are not, to get next to me, to sleep with me to change my mind because Parker paid you to do it?"

"That's not the way it was."

"Oh? Then what way was it, Brandon? Are you saying you didn't come here with me as your target, and our meeting had nothing to do with Parker wanting me to give up my controlling share of the company?"

Brandon felt the floor beneath him start to cave in, but he refused to lie. "Yes, but that changed once I got to know you."

That wasn't good enough for Cassie. She shook her head and began backing away from him. She felt both hurt and anger when she thought of all the time they had spent together, all the things they had done. And all of it had been nothing more than calculated moves on his part.

That realization filled her with humiliation. "You bastard! How dare you use me that way! I want you out of here. Out of my hotel," she all but screamed. "And you can go back and tell Parker that your mission wasn't accomplished. Hell will freeze two times over before I give him anything!"

It only took her a minute to snatch her boots off the floor and then she stormed past him and went to the sofa to grab her jacket and purse. Brandon was right on her heels.

"Listen, Cassie, please let me explain. I told Parker just now that I was going to tell you the truth."

She whirled on him. "You're lying!"

"No, I'm not lying, Cassie. I tried telling you the truth last night."

"It doesn't matter. You lied to me, Brandon, and I won't forget it. And I meant what I said. I want you out of my hotel or I will order that my staff put you out."

With that said and without taking the time to put on her boots, a barefoot Cassie opened the door and raced out of the suite.

Brandon studied the roadway as he drove toward Cassie's home, barely able to see due to the intense rain pouring down. By the time he had made it out of the suite after Cassie, she had gotten into her car and driven off. He had gone back inside and done as she'd demanded by packing, and within the hour he had checked out.

He had called his pilot to cancel his flight off the island. He refused to leave the Bahamas until he had a chance to talk to her again, to clear himself. Nothing mattered other than getting her to believe that although his intentions might not have been honorable when he'd arrived on the island, after getting to know her, he had known he could not go through with it. And he had tried telling her the truth last night.

But deep down he knew that none of that excused his behavior in her eyes. He also knew that she had a right to be angry and upset. He owed her an apology, which he intended to give her, and nothing would stop him from doing so. Not even the threat that Hurricane Melissa now posed since she had decided to head in this direction.

The hotel had been in chaos with people rushing to check out. No one wanted to remain on an island that was in the hurricane's path. But even with all the commotion, Cassie's staff had everything under control and was doing an outstanding job of keeping everyone calm and getting them checked out in a timely manner. For Cassie to be at home and not at the hotel was a strong indication of how upset she was and just how badly he had hurt her.

He inhaled a deep sigh of relief when he pulled into Cassie's driveway and saw her car was there. He hoped she had no intentions of going back out in this weather. From the report he'd heard on the car's radio, the authorities were saying it wasn't safe to travel and were asking people to stay off the roads since there had been a number of major auto accidents.

He glanced at her house when he brought the car to a stop. Judging the distance from where he was to her front door, chances were he would be soaked to the skin by the time he made it, but that was the least of his concerns. He needed to clear things up between them and he refused to entertain the thought that she wouldn't agree to listen to what he had to say.

He opened the car door and made a quick dash for the door. The forecasters still weren't certain if Hurricane Melissa would actually hit the island or just come close to crossing over it. Regardless of whether it was a hit or a miss, this island was definitely experiencing some of the effects of her fury. He was totally drenched by the time he knocked on Cassie's door. He had changed into a pair of jeans and the wet denim material seemed to cling to his body, almost squeezing him.

The door was snatched open and he could tell from Cassie's expression that she was both shocked and angry to see him. "I can't believe you have the nerve to come here."

"I'm here because you and I need to talk."

"Wrong, I have nothing to say to you and I would advise you to leave," she said, crossing her arms over her chest.

"We have a lot to say and I can't leave."

She glared at him. "And why not?"

"The weather. The police asked drivers to get off the road. If I go back out in that I risk the chance of having an accident."

Her glare hardened. "And you think I care?"

"Yes, because if there's one thing I've discovered about you over the past few days, it's that you are a caring person, Cassie, and no matter what kind of asshole you undoubtedly think I am, you would not send me to my death."

She leaned closer and got right in his face. "Want to bet?"

From the look in her eyes, the answer was no. At that particular moment he didn't want to bet, but he would take a chance. "Yes."

She glared at him some more. "I suggest that you go sit in your car until the weather improves for you to leave. You're not welcome in my home."

"If I do that then I run the risk of catching pneumonia in these wet clothes."

Evidently fed up with what she considered non-sense, she was about to slam the door in his face when he blocked it with his hand. "Look, Cassie, I'm not leaving until you hear me out, nor will I leave the island until you do. If you refuse to do so here today then whenever you go back to the hotel I'll make a nuisance of myself until you do agree to see me."

"Try it and I'll call the police," she snapped.

"Yes, you could do that, but imagine the bad publicity it will give the hotel. I'd think the last thing you'll want for the Garrison Grand-Bahamas is that." He knew what he'd said had hit a nerve. That would be the last thing she would want.

Except for the force of the rain falling, there was long silence as she stonily stared at him before angrily stepping aside. "Say what you have to say and leave."

When he walked across the threshold he glanced around and saw what she'd been doing before she'd come to answer the door. She had been rolling the hurricane shutters down to cover the windows. "Where's your staff?"

She glared at him. "Not that it's any of your business but I sent them home before the weather broke. I didn't want them caught out in it."

"But you have no qualms sending me back out in it," he said, meeting her gaze.

"No, I don't, so what does that tell you?" she stormed.

He crossed his arms across his chest and gave her a glare of his own. "It tells me that we really do need to talk. But first I'll help you get the shutters in place."

Cassie blinked. Was he crazy? She had no intention of him helping her do anything. "Excuse me. I don't recall asking for your help," she said sharply.

"No, but I intend to help anyway," he said, heading toward the window in the living room.

She raced after him. "I only let you in to talk, Brandon."

"I know," he agreed smoothly, over his shoulder. "But we can talk later. A hurricane might be headed this way and John would roll over in his grave if he thought I'd leave his daughter defenseless," he said, taking hold of the lever to work the shutter into place.

A puzzled frown crossed Cassie's brow and she stopped in her tracks. "You knew my father?"

He glanced over at her, knowing he would be completely honest with her from here on out and would tell her anything she wanted to know, provided it wasn't privileged information between attorney and client. "Yes, I knew John. I've known him all my life. He and my father, Stan Washington, were close friends, and had been since college."

He saw the surprised look in her eyes seconds before she asked, "Stan Washington was your father?"

"Yes. You'd met him?" he asked, moving to another window.

"I've known him all my life, as well," she said. "But I never knew anything personal about him other than he and Dad were close friends. He was the person Mom knew to contact if an emergency ever came up and she needed to reach Dad."

Brandon nodded. He figured his father had been. As close a friendship as the two men shared, Brandon had been certain his father had known about John's affair with Ava. Besides that, Stan had been the one who'd drawn up John's will and who had handled any legal matters dealing with the Garrison Grand-Bahamas exclusively. Once Cassie had taken ownership of the hotel she had retained her own attorneys.

"What about all the other windows?" he asked, after securing the shutters in place.

"I had my housekeeping staff help me with them before they left."

"Good," he murmured as he glanced over at her. She was still barefoot but had changed into a pair of capri pants and a blouse. And like everything else he'd ever seen on her body, she looked good. But then she looked rather good naked, too.

"Now you can have your say and leave."

His eyes moved from her body to her face. He had been caught staring and she wasn't happy about it, probably because she had an idea what thoughts had passed through his mind.

"I'd think my help just now has earned me a chance to get out of these clothes."

Her back became ramrod straight. "You can think again!"

He suddenly realized how that might have sounded. "Calm down, Cassie," he said, running his hand down his face. "That's not what I meant. I was suggesting it would be nice to get out of these wet things so you can dry them for me. Otherwise, I might catch pneumonia."

Cassie bit down on her lip to keep from telling him that when and if he caught pneumonia she hoped he died a slow, agonizing death, but then dished the thought from her mind. She wasn't a heartless or cruel person, although he was the last human being on earth who deserved even a drop of her kindness.

"Fine," she snapped. "The laundry room is this way," she said, walking out of the room knowing he had to walk briskly to keep up with her. "And I suggest you stay in that room until your clothes are dry."

"Why? Don't you have a towel I could use while they're drying?"

She shot a look at him that said he was skating on thin ice and it was getting thinner every minute. "I have plenty of towels but I prefer not seeing you parade around in one."

"Okay."

She abruptly stopped walking and turned to face him. "Look, Brandon. Apparently everything you've done in the last three days was nothing but a joke to you but I hope you don't see me laughing. You don't even see me smiling."

The humor that had been in Brandon's eyes immediately faded. When he spoke again his voice was barely audible. "No, I don't think the last three days were a joke, Cassie. In fact I think they were the most precious I've ever spent in my entire life. The only thing I regret is coming to this island thinking you were someone you are not and because of it, I screwed up something awful. The only thing I can do is be honest with you now."

She refused to let his words affect her in any way. There was no way she could trust him again. "It really doesn't matter what you say when we talk, Brandon. I won't be able to get beyond the fact that you deliberately deceived me."

"Not all of it was based on deceit, Cassie. When I made love to you it was based on complete sincerity. Please don't ever think that it wasn't."

"You used me," she flung out with intense anger in her voice.

He reached out and gently touched the cleft in her chin and said in a low voice, "No, I made love to you, Cassie. I gave you more of myself than I've ever given another woman, freely, unselfishly and completely. "

Knowing if she didn't take a step back from him she would weaken, she said, "The laundry room is straight ahead and on your right. And since you're so terrified of catching pneumonia, there's a linen closet with towels in that room. But I'm warning you to stay put until your clothes dry. I have enough to do with my time than worry about a half-naked man parading through my house. I need to fill all the bathtubs with water in case I lose electricity."

"And if you do lose electricity, the thought of being here in the dark won't bother you?"

"For your information, I won't be here. As soon as your clothes dry and you have your say, I'm going to the hotel to help out there."

"You're going out in that weather?" he asked in a disbelieving tone.

"I believe that's what I said," she said smartly.

"Weren't you listening when I said the authorities are asking people to stay off the streets?" he asked incredulously, refusing to believe anyone could be so pigheaded and stubborn.

She lifted her chin. "Yes, I was listening with as much concentration as you were when I was telling you to leave." She narrowed her eyes and then said, "Now if you will excuse me, I have things to do. When your clothes are dry and you're fully dressed again, you should be able to find me in the living room."

Narrowing his eyes, Brandon watched as she turned and walked away.

Cassie kept walking on shaky legs, refusing to give in to temptation and glance over her shoulder to look at Brandon once again. The man was unsettling in the worst possible way and the last thing she needed was having him here under her roof, especially when the two of them were completely alone.

She shook her head. At least he was taking off those wet jeans. She hadn't missed seeing how they had fit his body like a second layer of skin. She was glad he hadn't caught her staring at him when he had been putting the shutters up to the windows. Every time he had moved his body her eyes had moved with it. Not only had his wet jeans hugged his muscular thighs but they had shown what a nice tush he had, as well as a flat, firm stomach.

She sighed deeply, disgusted with herself. How could she still find the man desirable after what he had done? And she'd had no intention of accepting his help with the shutters but he hadn't given her a choice in the matter. He did just whatever he wanted. Even now his behavior and actions were totally unacceptable to her.

After filling up all the bathtubs and making sure there were candles in appropriate places and extra batteries had been placed beside her radio, she called the hotel. Simon had assured her that he had everything under control and for her to stay put and not try to come out in the weather. The majority of the people who had wanted to leave had checked out of the hotel without a hitch. The ones that had remained would ride the weather out at the Garrison Grand-Bahamas. If the authorities called for a complete evacuation of the hotel, then they would use the hotel's vans to provide transportation to the closest shelters that had been set up. Simon had insisted that she promise that if needed, she would leave her home and go to the nearest shelter, as well.

Satisfied her staff had everything under control, she walked into the living room, over to the French doors and glanced out. The ocean appeared fierce and angry, and the most recent forecast she'd heard—at least the most positive one—said that Melissa would weaken before passing over the Bahamas. But Cassie had lived on the island long enough to know there was also a chance the hurricane would intensify once it reached land as well.

She glanced up at the sky. Although it was mid-afternoon the sky had darkened to a velvet black and the clouds were thickening. Huge droplets of rain were drenching the earth and strong, gusty winds had trees swaying back and forth. She rubbed her arms, feeling a slight chill in the air. Even if Melissa did become a category four, Cassie wasn't afraid of losing her home. Her father had built this house to withstand just about anything.

*Except pain.*

It seemed those words filtered through her mind on a whisper. And she hung her head as more pain engulfed her, disturbed by the emotions that were scurrying through her. She drew in a deep breath, thinking she hadn't shed a single tear for what Jason had done to her, yet earlier today she had cried for the pain Brandon had caused her. Inwardly her heart was still crying.

Cassie lifted her head. She smelled Brandon's scent even before she actually heard him. She knew he was there and had known the exact moment he had entered the room. However, she wasn't ready to turn around yet, at least not until she had her full coat of armor in place. For a reason she was yet to understand, Brandon Jarrett Washington had gotten under her skin and even with all the anger she felt toward him, he was still embedded there.

"Cassie?"

She stiffened when the sound of his voice reached her. She tried ignoring the huskiness of his tone and the goose bumps that pricked her skin. Saying a silent prayer for strength, as well as the retention of her common sense, she slowly turned around. Because all the windows were protected by shutters, the room appeared slightly dark, yet she was able to make him out clearly. He stood rigid in the doorway and thankfully, fully dressed. He took a step into the room and heat coursed through her, and to her way of thinking she might have been thankful way too soon.

Although she didn't want to admit it, even in dry jeans and a shirt, Brandon looked the picture of a well-developed man. And she was reacting to his presence in a way she didn't want to and that realization was very disconcerting. The silence shrouding them within the room was a stark contradiction to the fury of the storm that was raging outside.

She tightened her hands into fists at her side when he slowly crossed the room to her. His gaze continued to touch hers when he reached out his hand to her and said in a soft voice, "Come, Cassie, let's sit on the sofa and talk."

# Seven

Cassie glanced down at the hand Brandon was offering her. That hand had touched her all over last night, as well as participated in their no-holds-barred lovemaking. Finding out about his betrayal had hurt and she wasn't ready to accept anything he offered her. She would listen to what he had to say and that would be it.

Refusing to accept his hand, she returned her gaze to his face and said, "You can sit on the sofa. I'll take the chair." Her lips tightened when she moved across the room to take her seat.

Brandon was still considering Cassie's actions just now when he headed toward the sofa. It was apparent she didn't intend to make things easy for him and he could accept that. He had wronged her and it would be hard as hell to make things right. He wasn't even sure it was something that could be done, but he would try. Nervous anxiety was trying to set in but he refused to let it. Somehow he had to get her to understand.

Once he was settled on the sofa he glanced over at her, but she was looking everywhere but at him. That gave him a chance to remember how she had looked that first night he'd seen her on the beach. Even before knowing who she was, he had been attracted to her, had wanted to get to know her, get close to her and make love to her.

He shifted in his seat. Intense desire was settling in his loins, blazing them beyond control. Now was not a good time for such magnetism and he figured if she were to notice, she wouldn't appreciate it. Not needing any more trouble on his plate than was already there, he shifted on the sofa again and found a position that made that part of his body less conspicuous, although his desire for her didn't decrease any.

"Before you get started would you like something to drink?"

He glanced up and met her gaze, surprised she would offer him anything. "Yes, please."

She left the room and that gave him a few moments to think. In a way it was a strange twist of fate that had brought him and Cassie together. Their fathers' friendship had extended from college to death and unless he cleared up this issue between them, he and Cassie could very well become bitter enemies. He didn't want that and was unwilling to accept it as an option.

She returned moments later with two glasses of wine, one for him and the other for herself. Instead of handing him his wineglass directly, she placed it on the table beside him. Evidently, she had no intention of them touching in any way. He picked up his glass and took a sip, regretting he was responsible for bringing their relationship to such a sorrowful state.

"You wanted to talk."

Her words reminded him of why she was there, not to mention the distinct chill in the air. He took another sip of his wine and then he began speaking. "As you know, the Garrisons didn't know about your existence until the reading of John's will. I'm not going to say that no one might have suspected he was involved in an affair with someone, but I think I can truthfully say that no one was aware that a child had resulted from that affair. You were quite a surprise to everyone."

When she didn't make any comment or show any expression on her face, he continued. "But what came as an even bigger surprise was the fact that John left you controlling interest to share with Parker. That was definitely a shocker to everyone, especially Parker, who is the oldest and probably the most ambitious of John's sons. It was assumed, as well as understood, that if anything ever happened to John, Parker would get the majority share of controlling interest. Such a move was only right since John had turned the running of Garrison over to Parker on his thirty-first birthday. And Parker has done an outstanding job since then. Therefore, I hope you can understand why he was not only hurt and confused, but also extremely upset."

He could tell by the look on Cassie's face that she didn't understand anything, or that stubborn mind of hers was refusing to let her. "As I told you earlier," he continued, "my father is the one who drew up John's will, so I didn't know anything about you until I read over the document a few days before I was to present the will to the family. Once I discovered the truth, I knew the reading of it wouldn't be pretty."

He took a deep breath and proceeded on. "Pursuing normal legal action in this case, we took moves to contest the will but found it airtight. And—"

"I guess Parker smartened up and thought twice about pushing for a DNA test, as well," she interrupted in a curt tone.

Brandon nodded. "Yes, I advised him that nothing would be gained from it. John claimed you as his child and that was that. Besides, there was no reason to really believe that you weren't. You and Parker made contact and he offered to buy out your share of the controlling interest. You turned him down."

"And that should have been the end of it," she snapped.

Brandon couldn't help the smile that touched the corners of his lips. "Yes, possibly. But that's where you and Parker are alike in some respect."

At the lifting of her dark, arched brow, he explained. "You're both extremely stubborn."

She narrowed her eyes at him. "That's your opinion."

He decided not to waste time arguing with her by telling her that was what he knew, especially after spending time with her. Although she and Parker had never officially met, the prime reason they didn't get along was because they were similar in a lot of ways. Besides being stubborn, both were ambitious and driven to succeed. Apparently John had recognized that quality in the both of them and felt together they would do a good job by continuing the empire he'd created.

"I'm waiting, Brandon."

He glanced over at Cassie and saw her frowning in irritation. "I want to apologize for assuming a lot of incorrect things about you, Cassie, and I hope you will find it in your heart to forgive me."

Cassie wasn't ready to say whether she would or would not forgive him. At the moment she was close to doing the latter. However, she was curious about something. "And just what did you assume about me?"

Brandon inhaled before speaking. "Before answering that, I need to say that when you decided to be a force to reckon with by not responding to my firm's letters or returning any more of Parker's phone calls, it was decided that I should come and meet with you and make you the offer in person. It was also decided that I should first come and see if I could dig up any interesting information on you and your past, to use as ammunition to later force your hand if you continued your refusal to sell."

By the daggered look she was giving him, he knew she was surprised he had been so blatantly honest. He could also tell she hadn't liked what he'd said. "You might be stubborn, Cassie, but I'm a man who likes winning. I'm an attorney who will fight for my clients, anyway that I can…as long as it's legal. Garrison Incorporated is my top client and I had no intention of Parker not getting what he wanted. My allegiance was to him and not to you."

Cassie straightened in the chair and leaned forward. Her eyes were shooting fire. "Forget about what's legal, Brandon. Did you consider what you planned to do unethical?" she snapped.

He leaned forward, as well. "At the time, considering what I assumed about you, no, I didn't think anything I had planned to do as being unethical. By your refusal to even discuss the issue of the controlling shares in a professional manner with Parker, I saw your actions as that of an inconsiderate, spoiled, willful, selfish and self-centered young woman. And to answer your earlier question, that's what I assumed about you."

That did it. Cassie angrily crossed the room to stand in front of him. With her hands on her hips, she glared at him. "You didn't even know me. How dare you make such judgments about me!"

He stood to face off with her. "And that's just it, Cassie. No one knew you and it was apparent you wanted to keep things that way, close yourself off from a family that really wants to get to know you. And if my initial opinion—sight unseen—of you sounds a bit harsh then all I have to say in my defense is that's the picture you painted of yourself to everyone."

Cassie turned her head away from him, knowing part of what he said was true. She'd still been grieving her mother's death when she'd gotten word of her father's passing. He had been buried without her being there to say her last goodbye and a part of her resented that, and had resented them for letting it happen. But then the truth of the matter was that they hadn't known about her, although she had known about them. They would not have known to contact her to tell her anything.

"Imagine my surprise," she heard Brandon say,

"when I arrived here and met you. You were nothing like any of us figured you to be. It didn't take long for me to discover that you didn't have an inconsiderate, spoiled, willful, selfish or self-centered bone in your body. The woman I met, the woman I became extremely attracted to even before I knew her true identity that night on the beach, was a caring, giving, humane and unselfish person."

He took a step closer to her when Cassie turned her head and looked at him. "She was also strikingly beautiful, vivacious, sexy, desirable and passionate," he said, lowering his voice to a deep, husky tone. "She was a woman who could cause my entire body to get heated just from looking at her, a woman who made feelings I'd never encountered before rush along my nerve endings every time I got close to her."

He leaned in closer. "And she's the woman whose lips I longed to lock with mine whenever they came within inches of each other. Like they are now."

An involuntary moan of desire escaped as a sigh from Cassie's lips. Brandon's words had lit a hot torch inside of her and as she gazed into his eyes, she saw the heated look she had become familiar with. And she couldn't help but take note that they were standing close, so close that the front of his body was pressed intimately against hers, and the warm hiss of his breath could be felt on her lips. Another thing she was aware of was the hardness of his erection that had settled firmly in the lower center of her body.

She shuddered from the heat his body was emitting. Luscious heat she was actually feeling, almost drowning in. And then there was the manly scent of him that was sending a primal need escalating through her. It was a need she hadn't known existed until she had met him and discovered that he had the ability to take her to a passionate level she hadn't been elevated to before.

She knew he was about to kiss her. She also knew he was stalling, giving her the opportunity to back up and deny what the two of them wanted. But that wasn't what she wanted. Although they still had a lot more talking to do, a lot more things to get straight, she felt at that particular moment that they needed time out to take a much needed break from their stress.

And indulge in a deliriously, mind-boggling kiss.

When to her way of thinking he didn't act quickly enough, she stuck out her tongue, and with a sultry caress, she traced the lining of his lips from corner to corner. She saw the surprise on his face and the darkening of his pupils just seconds before a deep guttural groan spilled forth from his throat. He reached out and wrapped his arms around her waist, and like a bird of prey, he swooped down and captured her lips with his.

He had a way of devouring her mouth with the finesse of a gazelle and the hunger of a wolf, sending shivers all the way through her. And when he began mating with her tongue with a mastery that nearly brought her to her knees, she released a moan deep in her throat.

He tasted of the wine he had drunk and had the scent of man and rain. And he was consuming her with such effectiveness that she could only stand there and purr. His kiss was turning her into one massive ball of desire and she felt a dampness form between her legs.

He pulled his mouth free. His breathing was heavy

when he said huskily, "If you don't want what I'm about to give you, stop me now, Cassie. If you don't, I doubt I'll be able to stop myself later."

She had no desire to stop him. In fact she intended to help. To prove her point, she pulled his shirt from where it was tucked inside his jeans, before freeing the snap and easing down his zipper. And with a boldness she'd only discovered she had last night, she slipped her hand inside his jeans and felt her fingers grip the rigid hardness of him. She cupped him, fondled him and felt him actually grow larger in her hand.

"I want to be inside of you, Cassie," he whispered hotly in her ear. "I want to feel your heat clamp me tight, squeeze me and pull everything I have to give out of me. I want to make love to you until neither of us has any energy left. And then, when we regain our strength I want to do it all over again. I want to bury myself inside you so deep, neither of us will know at what point our bodies are connected."

His erotic words sent fire flaming through her body. The dampness between her legs threatened to drench her thighs. "Then do it, Brandon. Do me. Now."

As far as Brandon was concerned, her wish was his command and he eased her down on the Persian rug with him and quickly began removing their clothes. The logical part of his brain told him to slow down, she wasn't going anywhere, but another part, that part that was throbbing for relief said he wasn't going fast enough.

When he had her completely naked he turned his attention to removing his own clothes. And she was there helping him by pulling his shirt over his head and tugging his jeans down his legs after she had removed his shoes and socks.

He made a low growl in his throat when she straddled him and began using her tongue to explore him all over, starting with the column of his neck. She worked her way downward, tasting the tight buds on his chest before easing lower and giving greedy licks around his navel. She left a wet trail from his belly button to where his erection lay in a bed of tight, dark curls.

Cassie paused only long enough to raise her head to look at Brandon before gripping the object of her desire in her hands again. Lowering her head, she blew a warm breath against his shaft before clamping her mouth over him. Then she simply took her time, determined to give him the same kind of pleasure he had given her last night.

His body arched upward, nearly off the floor, and he released a deep groan before reaching down and grabbing hold of her hair. She thought he was going to jerk her away from him. Instead he entwined his fingers in her hair and continued to groan profusely. And then he started uttering her name over and over from deep within his throat. The sound had her senses reeling and made the center part of her wetter than before.

"No more," he said, using his hands to pull her upward toward him to capture her lips. And then he was kissing her with a need she felt invading her body. And suddenly she found herself on her back, her legs raised over his shoulders, nearly around his neck. He then lifted her hips and before she could catch her breath, he swiftly entered her, going deep, embedding himself within her to the hilt.

And then he began those thrusts she remembered so well, she tried grabbing hold on his buns, but they were moving too fast, pumping inside of her too rapidly. So she went after the strong arms that were solid on both sides of her and held on to them.

Their eyes met. Their gazes locked. The only thing that wasn't still was the lower part of their bodies as he kept moving in and out of her, filling her in a way that had sweat pouring off his forehead and trickling down onto her breasts. And then she felt her body shudder into one mind-blowing orgasm, the kind that made her go wild beneath him while screaming out his name and digging her fingernails into his arms.

And then he threw his head back and screamed out her name, as well. She felt him explode inside of her and she clenched her muscles, pulling more from him and knowing what had just happened could have very well left her pregnant with his child if she weren't on the pill. But the thought of that didn't bother her like it should have because she knew at that moment, without a doubt, that she had fallen in love with him.

"The power's out."

Cassie's head snapped up when she felt a movement beside her. She quickly remembered where she was. On the floor in the living room in her home, naked. She had dozed off after making love to Brandon, several times and then some.

She squinted her eyes in the darkness, missing the warmth of his body next to hers. "I put the candles out. I just need to get up and light them."

"Can you see your way around in the dark?"

"With this I can," she said, reaching for a large flashlight nearby. She smiled. "I figured we might lose power so I was ready."

She turned the light toward him and, seeing his naked body, she deliberately aimed it on a certain part of him. She chuckled. "Does that thing ever go down?"

He grinned. "Not while you're around." He walked over toward her. "Where's your radio?"

"On that table over there."

"Let me borrow this for a second. I don't know my way around in your house in the dark as well as you do." He took the flashlight and slowly moved around the room. When he located the radio he turned it on. It was blasting a current weather report that turned out to be good news. The island had been spared the full impact of Melissa but another tropical island hadn't been quite as lucky. The worst of the storm was over and everyone without power should have it restored by morning.

Cassie crossed the room. "I want to call to make sure everything is okay at the hotel."

"All right. I'm going to get dressed and check to see how things are outside."

By the time Brandon returned he found Cassie in the kitchen. She had put back on her clothes and was standing over a stove…with heat. Seeing his raised brow she said, "Mom preferred gas when it came to cooking, so if nothing else, we won't starve."

He nodded as he leaned in the doorway. "How are things at the hotel?"

"Fine. The power went out but the generator kicked

in," she replied. "A few fallen trees but otherwise nothing major. How are things outside?"

"The same. A few fallen trees but otherwise nothing major. And it's still raining cats and dogs." He crossed the room to look into the pot she was stirring. "What are you cooking?"

She smiled up at him. "The conch chowder from the other night. I grabbed it out of the freezer. You said you liked it."

"I do. It's good to know you plan on feeding me."

She chuckled. "That's not all I plan to do to you, so I have to keep your strength up."

He came around and grabbed her from behind and pressed her against him. "For you I will always keep my strength up. What can I help you do?"

"Put the bowls and eating utensils on the table and pour some tea into the glasses."

Moments later they sat to eat and Brandon decided to use that time to finish the talk he had started earlier. "So now you know why I did what I did, Cassie. I'm not saying it was right." At her narrowed eyes he changed his strategy and said, "Okay, it was wrong but you weren't making things easy for anyone."

She leaned back in her chair. "Tell me, Brandon. What part of 'no' didn't Parker understand? No means no. He asked to buy me out and I said no, I wasn't interested. What was the purpose of him calling when my answer wasn't going to change?"

"The reason he refused to let up is because he's a staunch businessman, Cassie. Parker is a man who is used to going after what he wants, especially if it's something he felt was rightfully his in the first place. Besides, you never took the time to hear what he was offering."

"It would not have mattered. What Dad left me was a gift and there's no way I'd sell my shares, no matter how much Parker offered me. And if he keeps it up, you'll be representing him on harassment charges."

Brandon stared at her for a moment, knowing she was dead serious. He chuckled. She lifted a brow. "What's so funny?"

"You, Parker and all the other Garrison siblings, but specifically you and Parker. At first I wondered what the hell John was thinking when he put that will into place. Now I think I know, although I didn't before coming here and meeting you."

"Well, would you like to enlighten me?"

"Sure. Like I said earlier, you and Parker are a lot alike and I think John recognized that fact. Besides the fact that both of you are stubborn, the two of you have an innate drive to succeed. Apparently John recognized that quality in both of you and felt together you and Parker would do a good job by continuing the empire he'd started."

She shook her head. "That can't be it. Dad knew how much I loved it here. He of all people knew how I missed the islands while attending college in London. To do what you're insinuating would mean moving to Miami and he knew I wouldn't do that. I told him after returning from college that I would never leave the island again. It's my home and where I want to stay."

"Then why do you think he gave you and Parker sharing control?"

Cassie inhaled deeply. "I wished I knew the answer."

Brandon's face took on a serious expression before

he said, "Then hear me out on my theory. John loved all of his children, there's no doubt in my mind about that. I also believed that he recognized all of their strengths…as well as their weaknesses. Not taking anything away from the others, I think he saw you and Parker as the strongest link because of your business sense. Parker is an excellent businessman, a chip off the old block. He's done a wonderful job of running things while John was alive, so John knew of his capabilities. And I understand that you did a fantastic job managing the hotel, so he was aware of what you could do, as well. Personally, I don't think it was ever John's intent for you and Parker to share the running of Garrison, Inc. Both of your personalities are too strong for that and he knew it. I think he put you in place to serve as a check and balance for Parker whenever there's a need."

She gazed at him thoughtfully before saying, "If what you're saying is true then it would serve no purpose if I were to sell my share of control to Parker. I wouldn't be accomplishing what Dad wanted."

"No, you wouldn't."

She studied him for a moment. "You haven't forgotten that you're Parker's attorney, have you?"

He smiled as he shook his head. "No, and I wasn't speaking as Parker's attorney just now. I was speaking as your friend…and lover." After a brief moment, he said, "I'd like to make a suggestion."

"What?"

"Take a few days off and come to Miami with me. Meet Parker, as well as your other sisters and brothers. I know for a fact that they would love to meet you."

"I'm not ready to meet them, Brandon."

"I think that you are, Cassie. And I believe John would have wanted it that way. Otherwise, he would have given you ownership of the hotel and nothing else, but he didn't do that. He arranged it where sooner or later you would have to meet them. And why wouldn't you want to meet them? They're your siblings. Your family. The six of you share the same blood."

He laughed. "Hell, all of you certainly look alike."

She raised a surprised brow. "We do?"

"Yes. All of you have this same darn dimple right here," he said, leaning over and reaching out to touch the spot.

She tilted her chin, trying to keep the sensations his touch was causing from overtaking her. "It's a cleft, Brandon."

He chuckled, pulling his hand back, but not before brushing a kiss across her lips. "Whatever you want to call it, sweetheart."

His term of endearment caused a flutter in her chest and the love she felt for him sent a warm feeling flowing through her. A few moments passed and then she said in a soft voice, "Tell me about them."

Knowing her interest was a major step, Brandon bit back a smile. "All right. I think I've told you everything there is about Parker. He's thirty-six. No matter how arrogant he might have come across that time when you did speak to him, he's really a nice guy. He used to be a workaholic but things have changed since he's gotten married. His wife Anna is just what he needs. She was his assistant before they married."

He took a sip of his tea and then said, "Stephen is

thirty-five. Like Parker, he's strong-willed and dependable. He's also compassionate. He's married and his wife is Megan. They have a three-year-old daughter named Jade."

Cassie lifted her brow. "Correct me if I'm wrong but it's my understanding that he got married a few months ago."

Brandon smiled. "You are right."

"And he has a daughter that's three?"

Brandon chuckled. "Yes. He and Megan had an affair a few years ago and she got pregnant. He didn't find out he was a father until rather recently. Now they're back together and very happy."

A huge smile touched Brandon's lips when he said, "And then there's Adam. He and I share a very close friendship and I consider him my best friend. As a result, I spend more time with him than the rest. He's thirty and operates a popular nightclub, Estate. And last but not least are the twins, Brooke and Brittany. They're both twenty-eight. Brittany operates a restaurant called Brittany Beach, and Brooke operates the Sands, a luxury condominium building."

Cassie took a sip of her own tea before asking, "What about my father's wife?"

Brandon glanced at her over the rim of his glass. "What about her?"

"I'm sure she wasn't happy finding out about my mom," Cassie said.

Brandon put his glass down and met her gaze. "No, she wasn't. But finding out about you was an even bigger shock. A part of me wants to believe she had an idea that John was having an affair with someone, but I think finding out he had another child was a kicker. Needless to say, she didn't take the news very well."

Brandon decided not to provide Cassie with any details about Bonita, especially her drinking problem. He would, however, tell her this one thing. "If you decide to come to Miami with me, I want to be up front with you and let you know that Bonita Garrison won't like the fact that you there. Trust me when I say that it wouldn't bother her one bit if you decided to drop off the face of the earth."

Cassie almost choked on her tea. Once again Brandon had surprised her. Now that he had decided to tell her the truth about everything, he was being brutally honest. "If she feels that way then I'm sure the others—"

"Don't feel that way," he interrupted, knowing her assumptions. "Their mother doesn't influence how they treat people in any way. Come to Miami with me, Cassie, and meet them."

She ran her hands through her hair as she leaned back in her chair. "I don't think you know what you're asking of me, Brandon."

"And I think I do. It's the right thing to do. I know it and I believe you know it, as well. This bitter battle between you and Parker can't go on forever. Do you think that's what John would have wanted?"

She shook her head. "No."

"Neither do I." He paused, then he asked, "Will you promise that you will at least think about it?" He reached across the table and took her hand in his.

"Yes, I promise."

"And will you accept my apology for deceiving

you, Cassie? I was wrong, but I've told you the reason I did it."

She thought about his words. He had tried telling her the truth last night, and if sex was all he'd wanted from her, he'd had a good opportunity to get it the night she had invited him to her home for dinner. But he had resisted her advances. And even last night, she had been the one to make the first move.

She stared into his face knowing the issue of forgiveness had to be resolved between them. She could tell he was fully aware that he had hurt her and was deeply bothered by it. "Yes, now that you've explained everything, I accept your apology." She saw the relieved look that came into his eyes.

He hesitated a moment. "And another thing. I didn't use any protection when we made love, so if you're—"

"I'm not. I've been on the pill for a few years now, and I'm healthy otherwise."

Brandon nodded. "So am I. I just don't want you to think I'm usually so careless."

"I don't." She smiled, thinking of the way he handled their lovemaking, always making sure she got her pleasure before he got his. "In fact, I think you are one of the most precise men that I know."

Later that night Cassie lay snuggled close to Brandon in her own bed. She was on her side and he was behind her in spoon position, holding her close to the heat of him. The power had come back on a few hours ago and they had taken a shower together before going to bed and making love again.

He was sleeping soundly beside her, probably tired

to the bone. He had taken her hard and fast, and she had enjoyed every earth-shattering moment of it. Her body trembled when she remembered the mind-splitting orgasm they had shared. Brandon was undoubtedly the perfect lover.

And she appreciated him sharing bits and pieces about her siblings, satisfying a curiosity she hadn't wanted to acknowledge that she'd had. And then he had been completely honest with her about how her father's wife would probably feel toward her if she decided to do what Brandon had suggested and go to Miami with him.

She inhaled deeply. A part of her wanted to go and resolve this issue between her and Parker once and for all, and then another part didn't want to go. What if Brandon was wrong and they really didn't want to meet her like he thought?

Deciding she didn't want to bog her mind with thoughts of them anymore tonight she let her thoughts drift to the issue of her and Brandon. She knew that true love was more than a sexual attraction between two people. It was more than being good together in bed. It was about feelings and emotions. It was about wanting to commit your life to that person for the rest of your life.

It was about the things she and Brandon didn't have.

She loved him. That was a gimme. But she knew he didn't love her. He was attracted to her and he enjoyed making love to her. For him it had nothing to do with feelings and emotions. Her heart turned in her chest at the realization, but she couldn't blame him for lacking those things. He hadn't made her any promises. He hadn't offered her a commitment. She was okay with that. She had no choice.

Moments later when she discovered she couldn't get to sleep, she knew the reason why. She quietly eased out of bed, put on a robe to cover her naked body and slipped down the stairs. She entered the room where her parents' huge portrait hung on the wall and turned on the light. Whenever she had problems and issues weighing her down, she would come in here where she would feel their presence and remember happier times.

A few moments later she went to the aquarium, sat on a love seat and observed the many species of marine life in the tanks all around her. The sight and sound created a relaxing atmosphere and she sat there with her legs tucked beneath her and enjoyed the peaceful moments.

She left the aquarium a short while later and when she eased back in the bed, Brandon tightened his arm around her, pulled her closer to his warmth and whispered in her ear, "Where were you? I missed you."

She cuddled closer to him. "Umm, I went downstairs to think about some things."

"About what?"

"Whether I should go to Miami with you to meet my sisters and brothers and resolve the issue between me and Parker." She cupped Brandon's face in her hand. "I've decided to go, Brandon."

And then she leaned up and kissed him, believing in her heart that she had made the right decision.

# Eight

Cassie glanced over at Brandon, who was sitting across from her in his private plane. They had boarded just seconds ago and already his pilot was announcing they were ready for take off from the Nassau International Airport.

The last week had been spent preparing for this trip, both mentally and physically. As strange as it seemed, she was a twenty-seven-year-old woman who would be meeting her siblings, all five of them, for the first time. And surprisingly enough, once Brandon had told them of her decision to visit, she had heard from each of them…except for Parker. However, his wife Anna had contacted her and had seemed genuinely sincere when she'd said that she was looking forward to meeting her.

After remnants of Melissa's presence had left the island and the sun had reappeared, it was business as usual. Cassie had gone to the hotel that first day to check on things, and her other days she had spent with Brandon.

They had gotten the trees taken care of that had fallen on her property and then the rest of the time had been used taking care of each other. She'd given him a tour of the island and had introduced him to some of her mother's family. They had shopped together in the marketplace, had gone out to dinner together several times and had taken her parents' boat out for a cruise on the ocean. But her favorite had been the times she had spent in his arms, whether she was making love with him or just plain snuggling up close.

She would be spending two weeks in Miami as a guest in his home. After that, she would return to the Bahamas and resume her life as it had been before he'd entered it. She tried not to think about the day they would part, when he would go his way and she would go hers. In reality, they lived different lives. He had his life in America and she had hers in the islands.

And even now, she still wasn't sure of Brandon's feelings for her, but she was very certain of her feelings for him. She loved him and would carry that love to the grave with her. Like her mother, she was destined to love just one man for the rest of her life.

She continued to stare at Brandon, and as if he felt her eyes on him, he glanced up from the document he was reading and met her gaze. "You okay?" he asked, with concern in his voice, as he put the papers aside.

"Yes. I'm fine." And she truly was, because no matter how things ended between them, he had given her some of the best days of her life and she would always appreciate him for it.

"How about coming over here and sit with me."

She took a perusal of his seat. It couldn't fit two people. "It won't work."

He crooked his finger at her. "Come here. We'll make it work."

The raspy sound of his voice got to her and she unsnapped her seat belt and eased toward him. He unsnapped his own and pulled her down into his lap. "Don't be concerned with Gil," he said of his pilot. "His job is to get us to our destination and not be concerned with what's going on in here."

She snuggled into his lap, thinking this was what she would miss the most when he left—the closeness, the chance to be held tight in a man's arms, to be able to feel every muscle in his body, especially the weight of that body on hers. Not to mention the feel of him inside of her. Then there was his scent…it was one she would never forget. It was a manly aroma that reminded her of rain, sunshine and lots of sex.

"I spoke with Parker before we left."

She'd heard what he said but didn't respond. She was still thinking of lots of sex.

He tightened his arms around her as he glanced down. "Cassie?"

She tilted her head and looked up at him. "I heard you."

He didn't say anything for a moment, just reached out and softly caressed the cleft in her chin. She swallowed with his every slow, sensuous stroke. He was trying to get next to her. And it was working.

"What did he want?" she asked, forcing the words out from her constricted throat. His hand had moved from her chin and was now stroking the side of her face, the area right below her ear.

He pretended not to hear as he continued to trace a path from her ear to her neck. "Brandon?" she said, to get his attention.

"I heard you," he answered, meeting her gaze and grinning.

She grinned back. "What did Parker want?"

"He has summoned you to the compound for Sunday dinner."

She raised up and glanced at him with a perturbed look on her face. "He did what!"

He laughed. "I was joking. I knew you wouldn't like the word *summoned*. I like getting a rise out of you."

She eased her hands between his legs to his crotch. "I like getting a rise out of you, too. Now stop teasing and tell me what Parker wanted."

He pulled her hand back and drew her closer into his arms. "He wants to *invite* you to Sunday dinner at the Garrison Estate. It's a weekly affair for the Garrison family."

She nodded as she thought about what he'd said. "And what about Bonita Garrison? The woman who wouldn't care if I dropped off the face of the earth."

Brandon inhaled deeply. "I wondered about that myself, but knowing Parker he'll have everything under control."

Cassie glanced up at him. "You don't sound too convincing."

He lowered his head. "Maybe this will help," he

breathed against her lips while his hand lifted her skirt to stroke her thigh. He then stroked his tongue across her lips the same way his hand was massaging her thigh, gently, pleasurably and methodically. And if that wasn't enough, he inserted his tongue into her mouth and the impact shattered her nerve endings. Her lips parted on a sigh, which gave him deeper penetration, something he was good at taking advantage of. And he was doing so in a way that had her moaning from the sensations escalating through her. His exquisite tongue was doing wild and wonderful things to hers. Devouring her mouth. Deepening her desire.

"Buckle up for landing."

He lifted his head when his pilot's command came across the speaker. And then as if he couldn't resist, he lowered his head and kissed her again. This time it was Cassie who pulled back and whispered against his moist lips. "I think I need to go back to my own seat."

"Yes, you do," he agreed, tracing his tongue around her mouth before finally releasing her from his lap.

She eased back to her seat and quickly buckled in. She lifted her head. Their gazes met. She smiled. So did he.

The thought that suddenly ran though her mind was that they hadn't missed making love one single time since that first experience and they hadn't gone a day without sharing a kiss, either. Those would be memories that would have to sustain her. Memories she would forever cherish.

"Cassie?"

She glanced over at him. "Yes?"

"Welcome to Miami."

* * *

"Do you mind if I make a quick stop by my office to check on things?" Brandon asked Cassie as he drove his car down Ocean Drive. Her attention was on the happenings outside the car's window. During this time of the day, it wasn't unusual to spot models, vintage cars, Harleys and people on Rollerblades mixing in with the many tourists that visited South Beach.

She turned to him, smiling. The sun coming through the window seemed to place golden highlights in her hair. "No, not at all. I'm sure you want to check to make sure nothing was damaged during the storm, although from the looks of things, all this city got was plenty of rain."

"Which seem to have grown more people," Brandon said, chuckling. "This area gets more popular every day. Daytime is bad enough but wait until darkness falls and all the nightclubs open. South Beach becomes one big party land."

"Umm, sounds like fun."

He chuckled. "It is, and Adam's nightclub is right there in the thick of things. It's doing very well. Before you return to the Bahamas, I plan to make sure I take you out on the town one night, and Adam's club is just one of the many places we'll visit."

Cassie slanted a smile over at him. "Don't tell me you're one of those party animals."

He laughed. "Not anymore, but I used to be. Adam and I have a history of spending many a nights out partying and having a good time. We were intent on experiencing as much of the wilder side of life as we could. But after Dad's death I had to buckle down and get serious when everything fell on my shoulders. I will always appreciate your father for having faith in my abilities and retaining our firm after Dad died. John didn't have to do that, but by doing so, he gave me a chance to prove my worth."

Cassie nodded as her smile deepened. "So you settled down, but is Adam still the party animal?"

"Not to the degree he used to be," he said. "He's become a very serious businessman. You're going to like him."

"You would say that because he's your best friend," she said.

"Yes, but I think you're going to like all the Garrison siblings."

She gave him a doubtful look. "Even Parker?"

"Yes, even Parker. Once you get to know him you'll see he's really a nice guy, and like I told you before, his marriage to Anna has changed him in a lot of ways. He loves her very much. I would be the first to admit that I never thought I'd see the day he would settle down. After all, he was one of the city's most eligible bachelors, a status he liked having."

Cassie considered his words and wondered if there would ever be a woman in Brandon's life that he would fall in love with and want to marry and spend the rest of his life with.

"We're almost there, just another block. And you'll be able to see the Garrison Grand once I turn the corner. It's on one corner of Bricknell and my office is on the other."

No sooner had he said the words than she saw what had been her father's first hotel. A sense of pride flowed through Cassie. It was a beautiful high-rise, a stately structure.

"It's beautiful," she said, getting to study it in more detail when they came to a stop at a traffic light right in front of the grand-looking building. The Garrison Grand was a perfect name for it.

"Stephen's in charge of running it now and he's doing an excellent job. He has exemplary business skills, but he's going to have his hands full when the Hotel Victoria open its doors."

Cassie glanced at Brandon. "The Hotel Victoria?"

"Yes, it's a hotel that's presently under construction and is being built by Jordan Jefferies. It will be a competing hotel that will be slightly smaller in size but will rival the Garrison Grand in luxury and prestige and attract the same type of clientele. Jeffries is a shrewd businessman who can be rather ruthless at times. He's a person who's determined to succeed by any means necessary."

"Sounds a lot like Parker."

Brandon chuckled. "Yes, which is probably why the two can't get along. There's a sort of family rivalry going on between the Garrisons and the Jeffrieses and has been for a while. However, a couple of months ago, Brittany defied the feud and recently became engaged to Emilio, Jordan's brother."

"I can imagine Parker not being too happy about that," Cassie said.

"No, and neither is Jordan. But Brittany and Emilio seem very much in love and intend to live their lives the way they want without family interference."

"Good for them."

Brandon glanced over at her as he pulled the car to a stop in a spot in a parking garage. A name plate indicated the spot was designated for his vehicle only. "You sound like a rebel."

She unsnapped her seat belt, stretched over and placed a kiss on his lips. "I am. My mom told me how her family was against her dating my dad since he was a married man. She defied them and dated him anyway."

"What about you? Would you date a married man?"

She shook her head. "No, I'm more possessive than my mom ever was. I couldn't stand the thought of sharing. That's why I feel somewhat sympathetic to Bonita Garrison. I can only imagine how she must have felt finding out her husband had had a long-term affair with another woman. But then another part of me, the part that knew my father so well and knew what a loving and loyal man he was, feels there was a reason he sought love and happiness elsewhere."

Brandon shrugged. "Perhaps."

Cassie really didn't expect him to say any more than that. Even if he knew anything about her father and his wife's relationship, he wouldn't say. No matter what she and Brandon had shared, he was very loyal when it came to the Garrison family.

A few moments later they entered the lobby of the Washington Building. "My father purchased the land for this building over forty years ago from your father. At the time a young John Garrison, who was in his early twenties, was on his way to becoming a multimillionaire. He was single and one of the most eligible bachelors in Miami. My father was his attorney even then."

Cassie nodded as she glanced around before they stepped on the elevator. "Nice building."

"Thanks. My firm's office is on the twentieth floor," he said, pressing a button after the elevator door closed shut. "I lease out the extra office space to other businesses."

When the elevator came to a stop on the twentieth floor they began walking down a carpeted hall. Brandon's law firm's glass doors had his named written in bold gold script. The receptionist area was both massive and impressive, and a young lady who sat at the front desk smiled and greeted them when they entered.

Passing that area they rounded a corner that contained several spacious offices, where she noticed people working at their desks. Some looked up when she and Brandon passed their doors and others, who were busy working or talking on the phone, did not. Cassie figured since it was Friday, most were probably trying to bring their work week to an end at a reasonable time so their weekend could begin.

She admired the layout of the offices. She knew that every office was made up of three fundamental elements—architecture, furniture and technology— and it appeared that Brandon's firm emphasized all three. The interior provided a comfortable work environment where anyone would want to spend their working hours. The painted walls, carpeted floors in some areas and marble tile floors in others, modern furniture and state-of-the-art equipment all provided an upscale image of what she'd thought Brandon's place of business would be like and she hadn't been wrong.

"I should have warned you about my secretary,

Rachel Suarez," he said in a low voice. "She's been here for ages, started out as my dad's first secretary, and she thinks she owns the place. But I have to admit she does a fantastic job of running things. I have ten associates working for me and she keeps everyone in line, including my other thirty or so employees."

Cassie glanced over at him, not realizing his firm was so massive. "You have a rather large company."

"Yes, and they are good people and hard workers, every one of them."

"The layout is nice and no one is cramped for space," she openly observed.

Brandon's secretary's desk appeared to be in the center of things. The sixty-something-year-old woman's face broke into a bright smile when she saw her boss. "Brandon, I wasn't expecting you back until sometime next week."

He smiled. "I'm still officially on vacation. I just dropped by to see how everything faired during the storm."

The woman waved off his words with her hands. "It wasn't so bad. I'm just glad it didn't get worse. I understand the islands got more rain that we did."

She then glanced over at Cassie and gave her a huge smile. "Hello."

Cassie smiled back. "Hello to you."

Brandon began introductions. "Rachel, this is—"

"I know who she is," the woman said, offering Cassie her hand. "You look a lot like your daddy."

Cassie raised a surprised brow as she took the hand being offered. Her surprise had nothing to do with being told that she looked like her father since she knew that was true. Her surprise was that the woman knew who she was.

At Cassie's bemused expression Rachel explained. "I was Stan Washington's secretary when you were born."

Cassie nodded. In other words the woman had known about her parents' affair and, like Brandon's father, had been sworn to secrecy.

"I'm going to give Cassie a tour of my office, Rachel. And like I said, I'm still on vacation so I won't be accepting any calls if they come in."

Rachel grinned. "Yes, sir."

Brandon ushered Cassie down the carpeted hall to his office. When they entered he locked the door behind him. She only had time for a quick glance around before he pulled her into his arms. "Now to finish what we started on the plane," he said, before lowering his head for a kiss.

Their mouths had barely touched when Brandon's cell phone rang. Muttering a curse, he straightened and pulled it out of his pocket. He rolled his eyes upon seeing whose telephone number had appeared. "Yes, Adam?" he said, a split second from letting his best friend know he had caught him at a bad time.

"Yes, Cassie is here and yes, she's with me now." A few moments later he said. "No, she's not staying at the Garrison Grand. She'll be a guest in my home." He winked his eye at Cassie before she moved to sit on the sofa across the room, crossing her legs in a very sexy way.

"And, no," he continued, trying to concentrate on what Adam was saying and not on Cassie's legs, "you won't be able to meet her until dinner on Sunday. You might be my best friend but I can't let you use that fact to your advantage since Parker has requested that the family all meet her at the same time. Besides, I'm taking her to dinner tonight and tomorrow I plan to give her a tour of the town."

Brandon laughed at something Adam said and replied, "Okay, Adam. I'll let Cassie know." He then clicked off the phone and placed it back in his pocket.

"Let me know what?" she asked, returning to where he stood.

Brandon smiled. "If you want to go ahead and make him your favorite brother, he's fine with it."

A smile touched Cassie's lips. She had a feeing she was really going to like him. "He seems nice."

"He is. Like I told you, all of them are, including Parker. The two of you just rubbed each other the wrong way in the beginning."

"And what if he doesn't agree with the counteroffer I intend to make him? I want you to know that I won't back down. He can either take it or leave it."

Brandon grinned. Sunday dinner at the Garrisons would be interesting, as usual. "I wouldn't worry about it if I were you. Like I said, Parker is a sharp business-man and I believe he wants to end the animosity between the two of you and come up with a workable solution as much as you do."

He reached out and caressed the cleft in her chin. "Every time I touch this I get turned on."

Cassie smiled, shaking her head. "I think you get turned on even when you're not touching it."

He laughed. "That's true." And to prove his point he lowered his mouth and joined it with hers. Their lips locked. Their tongues mated. Desire was seeping into both of their bones. Brandon thought he would never get enough of this woman no matter how much he tried.

Moments later he lifted his head and drew back from the kiss, his gaze on her moist lips. "I better get you out of here. It's not safe to be in here alone with you. I've never made love to a woman in my office, but I might be driven to do that very thing with you."

On tiptoe she stretched up and brushed a kiss across his lips. In a way she wanted him to take her here. That way when they did go their separate ways, her presence would always be in here, a place where he spent the majority of his time working.

"Maybe not today, but promise you'll do it before I leave to return home."

He lifted a brow. "Do what?"

"Make love to me in here," she said, stepping closer and sliding her fingers to his nape to caress him there.

He released a shuddering sigh at her touch before asking, "Why would you want me to make love to you in here?"

"So you could always remember me, especially in here."

He was taken aback by her words, and then murmured softly, in a husky tone, "Do you honestly think I could forget you, Cassie? Do you think I'd be able to forget everything we've shared together?"

Before she could answer he bent his head and claimed her lips, kissing her with so much passion it made her stomach somersault. It made the lower part of her body feel highly sensitive to his very presence.

Reluctantly, he pulled his mouth away and gazed at her in a way that sent sensations rushing all through her. He took her hand in his. "Come on and let's get out of here before I do just what you ask and not care that I have an office full of people working today."

A smile touched his lips when he added, "They're a smart group of people who will get more than suspicious about all the noise we'll make."

"Umm, you think we'll make a lot of noise?" she asked when he unlocked the door.

"He glanced over at her before opening it and chuckled. "Sweetheart, we always do."

Later that night Cassie could feel the soft pounding of Brandon's heart against her back. His arms were wrapped around her as he slept. The warm afterglow of their lovemaking had lulled her to sleep, as well, but now she was awake.

And thinking.

He had a beautiful home, and after showing her around, she had felt the love he had for it while he'd given his tour. She had watched him carefully when he had shown her with pride the things that were his. They were possessions he had worked hard to get and he was still working hard to retain. He'd told her that a number of his father's clients had dropped his firm after his father's death, citing Brandon's youth and lack of experience. John Garrison had been one of the few who'd kept him on, and had gone even further by recommending him to others. With hard work Brandon had rebuilt the legacy his father had started.

When Brandon stirred in his sleep, she glanced over her shoulder and her gaze touched his sleeping face. She wanted him. She wanted to marry him. She wanted to have his babies. But most of all, she loved him. However, this would be one of those situations where she couldn't have any of the things she wanted.

Because he didn't love her in return.

And she could never spend her life with a man who didn't love her. She had grown up in an environment that was filled with too much love to want something less for herself.

She closed her eyes to blot out the advice her mind was giving her. *Get out while you can do so without getting your heart shattered. Take your memories and go.*

Cassie opened her eyes, knowing she would take the advice her mind was giving her. This was Brandon's world and hers was in the Bahamas. Instead of staying the two weeks she'd originally planned, she would let him know after dinner on Sunday that she would be leaving in a week. It was important that she and Parker resolved the issues between them, and she was looking forward to meeting her other siblings. After that it was time to move on. The more time she spent with Brandon, the more she yearned for things she could not have. Already her love for him was weakening her resolve and undermining her defenses.

It was time for her to make serious plans about returning home. There was no other way.

Brandon walked off the patio and back into his home to answer the ringing telephone. He stood in a spot where he could still see Cassie as she swam around in his pool.

The two-piece bathing suit she was wearing was sexual temptation at its finest, and he was quite content to just stand there and stare at her. But when his phone rang again, he knew that wasn't possible. He reached on the table to pick it up. "Yes?"

"Brandon, this is Parker."

He wondered when Parker would get around to calling him back. They had been playing phone tag for the better part of the day. He understood Parker had been in meetings most of yesterday, and Brandon and Cassie had left the house early this morning when he had taken her to breakfast and later on a tour of South Beach.

When she had mentioned that she had a taste for Chinese food, they had dined for lunch at one of his favorite restaurants, an upscale and trendy establishment called the China Grille. After lunch, instead of taking in more sights, he had done as she requested and had taken her to the cemetery where her father was buried. He had stood by her side when she'd finally got a chance to say goodbye and then he had held her in his arms while she cried when her grief had gotten too much for her.

Afterward, they had returned to his place to take a swim in the pool and relax a while before getting dressed for dinner and the South Beach night life.

"Yes, Parker, I'm glad we finally connected."

"I am, too. How's Cassie?"

Brandon turned and glanced out the bank of French doors to stare right at her. She was no longer in the water but was standing by the edge of the pool, getting ready to dive back in. It was his opinion—with the way she looked with the sunlight made the wet strands of her hair gleam, and her body made his breath catch every time he saw it, naked or in clothes—Cassie was every man's fantasy. That was definitely not something her oldest brother would appreciate hearing from him.

"Cassie's fine and is out by the pool. She wanted to take a swim before we go out to dinner."

"Everyone is looking forward to meeting her tomorrow," Parker said.

"Glad to hear it. I had a hard time convincing her of that, but I did, which is the main reason she's here in Miami."

"Just so you know, I haven't mentioned it to Mom."

Something in Parker's voice forced Brandon to ask, "But you will, right?"

"I don't think that will be a wise thing to do at this point."

Brandon didn't like the sound of that. Chances were Bonita would be home since she rarely left the house on Sundays. And, for that matter she was rarely sober after lunchtime, as well. "And why not, Parker? I've been totally up front with Cassie since she discovered our association and I'm not going to have her start doubting my word or intentions about anything. If Bonita will be at dinner tomorrow, before I agree to bring Cassie, I need a good reason why you won't be telling Bonita she's coming. That wouldn't be fair to either of them." He knew Cassie could hold her own against anyone, but in this particular situation, he felt she shouldn't be placed in a position where she had to.

For the next ten minutes Parker explained to Brandon why he'd made the decision he had, and after discussing it with his siblings, they felt Bonita being caught unaware would be the right approach to use. "That might be the right approach for Bonita, but what about Cassie? I can see an ugly scene exploding, one I don't like and wouldn't want to place her in."

Brandon rubbed his hand down his face. "I'm going to tell her, Parker, and explain things to her the way you have explained them to me. It's going to be her decision as to whether or not she still wants to come."

"And I agree she should know, which is the reason I wanted to talk to you. So when will you tell her?"

Brandon sighed deeply. "I'd rather wait until in the morning. I don't want anything to ruin the plans I have for dinner," he said, fighting for control of his voice. He still wasn't sure not telling Bonita was the right thing, although he understood Parker's reason for it.

"Please inform me of Cassie's decision one way or the other," Parker said. "If she doesn't want to join us for dinner at the Garrison Estate tomorrow evening, then we can all get together and take her out some-where else. Mom will wonder why we're not eating Sunday dinner at her place though, so either way, she's going to find out Cassie's in town and that we've made contact with her. I just think it's best if we all stand together and face Mom as a united front."

"I understand, Parker, but like I said, it will be Cassie's decision."

# Nine

Frowning, Cassie stared over at Brandon. "What do you mean Bonita Garrison doesn't know I was invited to dinner?"

Brandon sighed. He had known she would not like the news Parker had delivered yesterday. "Considering everything, the Garrison siblings felt it would be best if she didn't know," he explained.

From where he was standing, with his shoulder propped against the bookshelves in his library, he could tell that Cassie, who was sitting on a sofa, was confused by that statement.

"But it's her house, right?" she asked, as if for clarification.

"Yes, it's her house."

"Then am I to assume she's out of town or something and won't be there?"

"No, you aren't to assume that." He saw the defiant look in her eyes, a strong indication as to what direction this conversation was going.

"Then I think you need to tell me what's going on, Brandon."

He sighed again, more deeply this time. What he needed was a drink, but that would have to come later. He really did owe her an explanation. Straightening, he crossed the room to sit beside her on the sofa. His gaze locked on her face when he said, "Bonita Garrison is an alcoholic and has been for years. She's always had a drinking problem and John's will only escalated the condition. Like I told you before, considering the state of their marriage, I think she had an idea he was having an affair, but she didn't know anything about you. That was one well-kept secret."

Cassie's frown deepened. "Have any of her children suggested that she seek professional help?"

"Yes, countless times. I understand John even did so, but for the longest she wouldn't acknowledge she had a problem. She still hasn't."

Cassie nodded. "But what does that have to do with me? Wouldn't seeing me in her home uninvited, the person who is living proof of her husband's unfaithfulness, push her even more over the edge?"

He reached for her hand. "Parker and the others are hoping it doesn't. Their relationship with her is strained and has been for some time. I'm talking years, Cassie. They'd decided, and unanimously I might add, that they want to meet you, build relationships with you, include you in the family mix, and they refused to sneak behind their mother's back to do so. They believe it's time to mend the fences and move on, and want Bonita to see that as a united group they plan to do just that, with or without her blessings."

He chuckled. "I've known those Garrisons most of my life and this is the first time they've ever been in complete agreement about anything."

Brandon got quiet for a moment and then said in a serious tone, "John would be proud of them. And knowing the type of man he was, a man who loved his children unconditionally, I want to believe that had he lived, he would have eventually gotten all of you together. He was a man who would have made it happen."

His words had Cassie staring at him thoughtfully. What he'd said was true. She believed that, as well. She had learned about her siblings' existence from her father, and she had known he had loved them as much as he had loved her. He had said so a number of times.

"But…" she said, frowning still. "What if things get ugly?"

"And there's a possibility that they might," he said honestly, needing to make her aware of that fact. "But Parker wants you to know that no matter what, they intend to finally bring things to a head, a forced-feeding intervention, so to speak."

Cassie inhaled a deep breath. She just hoped Parker and the others were right. The last thing she wanted was to be responsible for Bonita Garrison getting pushed over the edge. But then her children knew her better than anyone and Cassie was sure that no matter how strained their relationship, that they loved their mother. And if they felt what they had planned for this afternoon was the right approach to use then she would trust their judgment.

She met Brandon's gaze. "Okay, thanks for telling me."

"Are you still going?"

"Yes. I'm going." After a moment, she asked, "You will be there, too, right?"

A smile touched the corners of his lips. "Yes, I was invited, as well, and I will be there," he said. Tugging on the hand he still held he pulled her closer to him and whispered, "But even if I weren't invited I would still be there, Cassie. You would not be alone."

Cassie glanced around when Brandon brought the car to a stop in front of the massive and impressive Spanish-style villa that was the Garrison Estate. Everywhere she looked she saw a beauty that was spellbinding. From the brick driveway to the wide stucco stairs that led to the entrance, she thought there weren't many words that could be used to describe the house that could sufficiently do it justice.

She inhaled a reverent breath in knowing this is where her father had lived, the place he considered home when he wasn't in the Bahamas with her and her mom. And even now a part of her could feel his presence. What Brandon had said earlier that day was true. Her father would want his offspring to meet.

"You've gotten quiet on me. Are you okay?"

She glanced over at Brandon, hearing the concern in his voice. From the moment his plane had landed in Miami, he had been attentive, considerate of her well-being and so forthcoming with his affection. More than once she'd had to stop and remind herself that his affection had nothing to do with love, but was a result of his kindness. There was a natural degree of warmth and caring about him. Those were just two of the things that had drawn her to him from the first.

"Yes, I'm okay. I was just thinking about Dad and how much I loved him and how much I miss him, and how today I can feel his presence more so than ever."

"And you never resented him for having another family besides you and your mom?"

"I never resented Dad, but when I was a lot younger, after having found out he was a married man with another family, for a long time I resented them. In my mind, whenever he would leave me and Mom it would be to return here to them. I never gave thought to the fact that whenever he was in the Bahamas with me and Mom, he wasn't with them, either. I was too possessive of him in my life to even care."

"But now?"

"But now I want to believe that somehow he was able to give all six of us equal time, special time, as special as he was," she said softly.

"I think he did," Brandon said in a quiet tone. "I believe he knew what each of his kids needed and gave it to them. He was an ingrained part of each of their lives and they loved him just as much as you did."

Her eyebrows lifted. "Do you think that even now? After finding out he'd had a long-term affair while married to their mother? You don't think that love was tarnished because of it?"

Brandon shook his head. "No. Adam is the only one

I've spoken to in depth about it, basically to garner his personal feelings. He said they all knew their parents' marriage was on the rocks for years. Bonita's abuse of alcohol led to a friction that couldn't be mended."

Cassie nodded, then dragged in a deep breath and said, "It's time we go inside, isn't it?"

"Yes. Nervous?"

"I would be lying if I were to say no. But I can handle it."

Brandon chuckled as he unbuckled his seat belt. "Cassie Sinclair-Garrison, I think you can handle just about anything."

He exited the car and came around to open her door for her, admiring what she was wearing. Although it was the middle of fall, the weather was warm and the sky was clear and she was casually dressed in a pair of black slacks and a velvet plum blouse. The outfit not only brought out the natural beauty of her skin coloring, but added a touch of exuberance to her brown eyes, as well. She smiled at him.

He offered his hand and she took it. The sensation that immediately flowed through him was desire that was as intoxicating as the strongest liquor.

After closing the door, he placed her hand on his arm and walked her up the wide stucco stairs that led to the front door. Before he could raise his hand to knock, the door opened and Lisette Wilson stood there smiling at them. The woman had been the Garrison's housekeeper for as long as Brandon could remember and, according to Adam, Lisette was a force to reckon with when he'd been going through his mischievous teen years. Now she seemed older, and although a smile was bright on her face, she looked tired. She was probably worn out from having her hands full these days with Bonita's excessive drinking. With none of the Garrison siblings living at home, they depended on Lisette to keep things running as smoothly as possible on the home front.

"Mr. Brandon, good seeing you again, and I want to welcome the both of you to the Garrison Estate."

Brandon returned the woman's smile. "Thanks, Lisette. Have Parker and the others arrived yet?"

"Yes, they're on the veranda," she said, stepping aside for them to enter. "I'll take you to them."

Lisette led the way. Brandon could feel the tenseness of Cassie's hand on his arm. He smiled over at her as they passed a wide stone column that marked the entrance to the living room. After passing through several beautifully decorated rooms, they walked through a bank of French doors to the veranda. The Garrison siblings were there. All five of them. Along with three of their significant others.

"Your dinner guests have arrived," Lisette announced.

The group immediately ended whatever conversation they were engaged in and turned, seemingly all at once. Eight pairs of eyes stared at them, mainly at Cassie. They appeared stunned. The look on their faces confirmed that they were thinking what Brandon already knew. She was definitely a Garrison.

It was Parker who made the first move, crossing the veranda with an air that was cool and confident. He came to a stop in front of them. He continued to stare at Cassie, studying her features, probably with the same intensity that she was studying his.

For her it was like seeing what she figured was a younger version of their father. He looked so much like John Garrison it was uncanny. All three Garrison men did. That was the first thought that had crossed her mind when they had looked at her. But Parker, the first-born, had acquired nearly every physical feature their father had possessed, including his height, build and mannerisms—especially how his dark brow creased in a deep, thoughtful frown when he analyzed anything.

Not feeling at all intimidated, Cassie tilted her head back as she met his intense stare. Then she watched his eyes soften speculatively when he said, "Umm, the famous Garrison cleft. Was there ever a time you thought it was a curse rather than a blessing?"

Refusing to let her guard down, not even for a second, Cassie said, "No, that never occurred to me. Anything I inherited from my father I considered a blessing."

A semblance of a smile touched his arrogant lips and he said, "So did I." Extending his hand out to her, he said, "I'm Parker, by the way."

She accepted it. "And I'm Cassie."

He nodded before glancing over at Brandon. "Good seeing you again, Brandon."

"Likewise, Parker."

Parker's eyes then returned to Cassie. "There's a group of people who're anxious to meet you. Please come and let me introduce them."

"All right," she said, giving Parker the same semblance of a smile that he'd given her as she held his gaze steadily. Their opposing wills seemed to be squaring off, but in a sociable way. "I'd love to meet everyone," she said.

Cassie glanced over at Brandon and he smiled at her, and immediately his strength touched her, gave her the added confidence she needed. She fell in love with him even more.

She inhaled deeply as the two men escorted her across the veranda to meet the others. As much as she didn't want them to be, butterflies were flying around in her stomach at the round of introductions she was about to engage in.

She forced herself to relax and smiled when they came to a stop before a woman she quickly assumed to be Parker's wife, from the way he was looking at her. He might have been a happy bachelor at one time, but from the way he gently placed an arm around the beautiful woman with shoulder-length dark hair and green eyes, it was quite easy to tell he was a man very much in love.

He smiled affectionately at his wife before returning his gaze to Cassie. "Cassie, I'd like you to meet my wife, Anna."

Instead of shaking her hand, Anna gave her an affectionate hug. "It's nice meeting you, Cassie, and welcome to the family."

"Thank you."

Without taking more than a step, Cassie came to stand in front of two men she immediately knew were her other two brothers, since their clefts were dead giveaways. The woman standing between them had green eyes and wavy red hair. And just like Parker's wife, she was gorgeous.

"Cassie, welcome to Miami and I'm Stephen," the man standing to her left said, making his own introductions while slanting a smile at her and taking the hand she offered. "And this is my wife, Megan."

Like Anna, Megan automatically reached out and hugged her. "It's nice to finally get to meet you," Megan said, smiling at her with sincerity in her eyes. "And you have a three-year-old niece name Jade who I'm hoping you'll get to meet before you return to the Bahamas."

"I would love that and can't imagine leaving Miami before I do."

She then glanced at the other man, who was tall, dark and handsome—common traits, it seemed, with Garrison men. "And you must be Adam," she said.

A broad grin flitted across his face and suddenly two words came to her mind regarding him—loyal and dedicated. He reached out and gave her a hug and a kiss on the cheek. "Yes, I'm Adam, and remember, I'm to be the favorite brother."

She met his gaze and had a feeling that he would be. "I'll remember that."

She then turned and saw two women and a very handsome man of Cuban descent. She knew immediately that the two women were her identical twin sisters.

"Cassie, I'd like you to meet Brooke, the oldest of the twins by a few minutes," Parker said of the tall, attractive, model-thin woman with long dark brown hair and brown eyes. "And this is Brittany and her fiancé, Emilio Jeffries."

Cassie faintly raised a brow at the derision she'd heard in Parker's voice when he had introduced Emilio. She then remembered what Brandon had shared with her about there being bad blood between the Garrisons and the Jefferieses, and how Brittany had basically fallen in love with one of her brother's enemies. But still, she couldn't help but admire

Brittany for her bravery, as well as her good common sense. No woman in her right mind would let a hunk like Emilio slip through her fingers, regardless of how her family felt about it.

"It's nice meeting all of you," Cassie said, glancing around at everyone and very much aware of the moment Brandon came to stand next to her side.

"It's good to know I'm no longer the baby in the family," Brittany said, grinning.

The next few minutes Cassie mingled with everyone while answering numerous questions about her life in the Bahamas, without any of the inquiries getting specific about the relationship between their father and her mother. Stephen asked about the activities at the Garrison Grand-Bahamas and complimented her on the great job she was doing.

For the most part Parker didn't say anything, and knowing the astute businessman that he was, she figured he was hanging low and listening for any details regarding her business affairs that might interest him.

"Dinner is ready to be served."

Everyone glanced over in Lisette's direction before the woman disappeared back inside.

"Would you give me the honor of escorting you in to dinner?" Adam asked as he appeared at her side. "I'm sure Brandon won't mind," he added, winking an eye at the man he considered his best friend.

Cassie smiled serenely, wondering how much her siblings knew…or thought they knew of her and Brandon's relationship. Did they assume they were friends, lovers or what? Did she care? She knew the terms of their relationship, the boundaries as well as the life span of it.

She smiled over at Brandon before returning her gaze to Adam. Before she could open her mouth to say anything, she felt Brandon's hand at her back when he said in a low tone, "I think we will both do the honor, Adam. I've appointed myself her escort for the evening."

She saw the two men exchange meaningful looks. She was aware, as much as they were, that Bonita Garrison had not yet made an appearance. "I think having two escorts is a splendid idea," she said.

When they reached the dining room she noted Parker had taken the chair at the head of the table. Brandon took the chair on one side of her and Adam took a chair on the other side. Emilio was sitting across from her and they shared a smile. She suspected that he felt as much an outsider as she did. There was the easy and familiar camaraderie the others shared, including Brandon. He'd evidently shared Sunday dinner with the group before because he seemed to be right at home.

"So when can I come visit you in the Bahamas?" Brooke asked, smiling over at Cassie.

Before she could respond, Adam said, "Trying to get the hell out of Dodge for some reason, sis?"

She rolled her eyes at him. "Not particularly," she said, not meeting his gaze as she suddenly began concentrating on the plate Lisette set in front of her.

"You're welcome to visit me any time," Cassie said and meant it. When Brooke glanced up, Cassie could have sworn she'd seen a look of profound thanks in her eyes. That made Cassie wonder if perhaps what Adam had jokingly said was true and Brooke was trying to escape Miami for a reason.

Conversation was amiable with Adam, Brooke and Brittany telling her about the establishments they owned and ran under the Garrison umbrella. Stephen discussed the Miami Garrison Grand and even asked her advice on a couple of things that he'd heard she had implemented at her hotel.

When Brooke excused herself for the second time to go to the bathroom, Cassie overheard Brittany whisper to Emilio that she thought her twin was pregnant. Cassie was grateful everyone else had been too busy listening to Megan share one of her disastrous interior decorating experiences to hear Brittany's comment.

Suddenly, the dining room got deathly quiet and Cassie knew why when Brandon reached for her hand and held it tight in his. She followed everyone's gaze and glanced at the woman who was standing in the entrance of the dining room. Regardless of what curiosity she had always harbored about her father's wife, she never in a million years thought such disappointment would assail her body like it was doing now.

It was easy to see that at one time Bonita Garrison had been a beautiful woman, definitely stunning enough to catch a young John Garrison's eye. But the woman who appeared almost too drunk to stand up straight while holding a half-filled glass of liquor in her hand looked tired and beaten.

"Mother, we weren't sure you would be joining us," Parker said, standing along with all the other men at the table.

"Would it have mattered?" Bonita snapped, almost

staggering with each step she took. She made it to the chair on the other side of Parker and sat.

Resuming his seat, Parker glanced at Lisette, who had entered, and said, "Please bring my mother a plate as well as a cup of coffee."

The woman glared at her oldest son. "I don't need anything to drink, Parker. I have everything I need right here," she said in a slurred voice, saluting her glass at him.

"I would say you've had too much, Mom."

The comment came from Stephen and whereas Bonita Garrison had glared at Parker just moments earlier, she actually smiled at Stephen. She didn't say anything to Stephen directly, but instead announced, "Maybe I'll have a cup of coffee after all."

Cassie knew it was then that Bonita noticed her presence. She saw Brandon sitting beside her and holding her hand, and said, "Brandon, how nice, you've brought a date."

Brandon didn't say anything but merely nodded, while Bonita continued to stare. Cassie figured that it wouldn't take long before her identity became obvious with her sitting so close to Brittany. Other than the color of their skin, the two women favored. In her drunken state such a thing could go over Bonita's head.

But it didn't.

Cassie found herself the object of the woman's intense attention and then suddenly Bonita rose on drunken legs and, not speaking to anyone in particular, she asked, "Who is she?"

It was Parker who spoke. "Cassie. Cassie Sinclair-Garrison."

The woman snatched her gaze from Cassie and glared at Parker. "That woman's child? You invited that *woman's* child to our home?"

"No, I invited our *father's* child to our home, Mother. Cassie is our sister and we thought it was time we met her," Parker answered with the same mastery in his voice that Cassie was certain he used in the boardroom.

Bonita's features took on a stony countenance. "Meet her? Why would you want to meet her after what your father and her mother did to me?"

"Whatever happened between you and Dad was between you and Dad," Adam said firmly, his jaw set.

"And no matter what happened, Mother, or the participants involved, nothing changes the fact that Cassie *is* our sister and we want to get to know her," Stephen added.

Bonita slowly glanced around the table and saw a look of conformity on the faces of Brooke and Brittany as well. Angrily, she slammed her glass down. "Don't expect me to be happy about it." She then stormed out the room.

"Maybe we should consider cancelling her sixtieth birthday party," Brittany said softly.

No one agreed or disagreed. Instead, Parker met Cassie's gaze and said, "I want to apologize for my mother's behavior."

Cassie shook her head. "You don't have to apologize. I just regret upsetting your mother."

"Don't sweat it," Adam said, smiling as he took a sip of his wine. "Everything upsets Mother. We're used to it and have been for a long time. Over the years we've learned to deal with it. Some better than others."

Dinner resumed and the tension eventually passed. Cassie, like everyone else, indulged in the shared discussions, murmurs, chuckles and laughter around the table. Feeling more comfortable, she began to relax and more than once she glanced over at Brandon to find him staring at her.

When dinner was over everyone retired to the family room. Moments later, Brandon asked to speak with Parker privately. She knew he would be telling them of her wish not to discuss any business today, and that she preferred meeting with Parker tomorrow.

Moments later, she found herself alone with Brittany, Brooke and Emilio. Anna and Megan, who were close friends, took a walk outside to admire one of the many flower gardens surrounding the estate, and Stephen and Adam had excused themselves to speak with Lisette.

"I see your brother still doesn't care for me," Emilio said, chuckling to Brittany.

She leaned up and kissed his cheek. "Doesn't matter, since I like you."

Fascinated, Cassie decided to ask, "Do you think he'll ever soften up?"

Brooke lifted an arched brow. "Who, Parker? No. That would be too easy," she said, with more than a trace of annoyance in her voice.

"And he's really upset now that he knows that Jordan has acquired a piece of land he had his sights on," Emilio said. Then since he thought Cassie didn't know, he added, "Jordan is my brother."

"Excuse me, please. I think I'll join Anna and Megan in getting some fresh air," Brooke said rather tersely before turning and walking out the French doors.

Brittany watched her twin leave. "I wonder what that was about?" she said thoughtfully. "Something's up with her."

"Pure speculation on Brittany's part," Emilio added. "She thinks Brooke's been acting strange lately."

"It's not what I think, sweetheart. It's what I know. She's my twin, so I can't help but notice certain things."

Before Brittany could speculate any further, Brandon, Parker, Stephen and Adam returned. Brandon came up to her and slipped his hand around her waist. "Ready to leave?"

Cassie smiled up at him. "Yes, if you are."

She promised Brittany she would drop by her restaurant this week and gave Brooke her word she would visit the condominiums that Brooke owned.

Before leaving she made more promises. Adam wanted her presence at his club at least once and Stephen asked her to come by the Garrison Grand so he could give her a tour. Parker hadn't asked her to promise him anything since he was meeting with her first thing in the morning at his office. The most important thing to him was for them to come together and find a resolution to what was keeping them at arm's length.

When she and Brandon walked to the car she smiled over at him. "Dinner wasn't so bad."

He grinned. "No, I guess not. What did you think about Bonita?"

"I hope that she'll get professional help, and soon."

"What about your siblings?"

She tilted her head and said, "To be quite honest, I like them."

He opened the car door for her. "I told you that you would. Even Parker softened up some."

When he came around and got inside the driver's side he glanced at his watch. "I know just the place I want to take you now."

She glanced over at him upon hearing the sensual huskiness of his tone. "Oh, really? Where?"

"My office."

# Ten

After walking down the carpeted hallway holding hands, they reached Brandon's office. There was no guesswork as to why they were in an empty office on a Sunday night.

Cassie could unashamedly remember her request to him a couple of days ago, and there was no doubt in her mind that he was going to give her just what she'd asked for.

She chewed her bottom lip, not in nervousness but in anticipation. Goose bumps had begun forming on her arms, desire was making her panties wet and her tongue ached to mingle with Brandon's in a hot-and-heavy kiss. From the time he had announced just where he would be taking her and they had pulled out of the brick driveway of the Garrison Estate, sensations, thick and rampant, had flowed through her, making her shift positions in her seat a few times.

Cassie's thoughts shifted back to the here and now when Brandon released his hold on her hand and she immediately felt the loss of his touch. Opening the office door, his touch was back when he guided her inside before closing the door behind them. He tugged on her hand and brought her closer to him.

She felt weak in the knees, and to retain her balance, she placed her hands on his chest and gazed up at him, remembering the last time they had made love. It had been early that morning when they had awakened. And his lovemaking last night had given her a good night's sleep and been the very thing that had lulled her awake that morning as well. She'd wanted more of what he had the ability to give her. He had been more than happy to oblige her in the most fervent and passionate way.

She knew she should tell him of her decision to return to the Bahamas sooner than she'd originally planned, but at the moment she couldn't. The only thing she could do while standing in his embrace was get turned on even more by the gorgeous brown eyes looking down at her. Being the sole focus of his attention was causing all sorts of emotions to run through her; feelings that were intimate and private, feelings that could only be shared with him.

"Do you know what I think about whenever I look at you?" Brandon asked in a low husky voice, taking his forefinger and tracing the dimple in her chin.

She shook her head. She only knew what she thought about whenever she looked at him. "No. Tell me. What do you think when you look at me, Brandon?"

He took a step back and his gaze flicked over her from head to toe, and then he met her eyes. "I think about stripping you naked and then kissing you all over. But I want to do more than just kiss you. I want to taste you, to savor your flavor, get entrenched in your heated aroma, and to get totally enmeshed in the very essence of you."

Cassie was caught between wanting to breathe and not wanting to breathe. His words had started her heart to race in her chest and was making heat shimmer through all parts of her. Whenever they made love he had the ability to let go and give full measure, holding nothing back and making her the recipient of something so earth-shattering and profound.

With a heated sigh, she recovered the distance he had placed between them and reached out and wrapped her arms around his neck. She stared into his face, studied it with the intensity that only a woman in love could do, taking in every detail of his features—the dark brown eyes, sensual lips and firm jaw. Despite her determination to return to the island and live her life alone, she knew there was no way she would ever forget him and how he made her feel while doing all those wonderful things to her.

"On Friday you said you wanted me to make love to you in here because you didn't want me to forget you. Why do you think I'd forget you, Cassie?"

Chewing her bottom lip, she met his gaze knowing his inquiry demanded an answer, one she wasn't ready to share with him. If she did, she would come across as a needy person, a woman wanting the love of a man who wasn't ready to give it. A man she figured had no intention of ever getting married after what his fiancée had done to him. But then, hadn't she figured that same thing about her own life after Jason?

"Cassie?"

Giving him an answer that was not the complete truth she said, "Because I know this is just a moment we are sharing, Brandon, and nothing more. I know it and you know it, as well. But I want you to remember me like I will always remember you. And since this is where you spend a lot of your time, I want you to remember me here."

He smiled with a touch to his lips that made more heat flow through her. "Especially in here?" he asked in a deep, throaty voice.

"Yes, especially in here," she replied silkily. "I want to get into your mind, Brandon." What she wouldn't say is that she wanted to get in his heart, as well, but she knew that was wishful thinking.

With all amusement leaving his face, he said in a serious tone and with a solemn expression, "You *are* in my mind, Cassie."

She swallowed. She had all intention of making some kind of sassy comeback, but didn't. She so desperately wanted to believe him, and in a way she did believe him. He might not be in love with her, but over the past couple of weeks they had bonded in a way that went beyond the bedroom. He had come to the island seeking her out with a less than an honorable purpose, but in the end he had come clean and had been completely truthful with her, telling her more than she'd counted on.

And he had brought her here tonight to make the

memories she wanted him to have, even when she would be across the span of an ocean from him, he would remember her in here. The happiness she felt at that moment made her feel light-headed and she automatically breathed air into her lungs, picking up his manly scent in the process. "Then let's make memories, Brandon. Let's make them together."

Brandon stared at Cassie. He wanted her with a desperation he almost found frightening. The intensity of his desire was almost mind-boggling. It had been that way each and every time they made physical contact. She was an itch he couldn't scratch enough, a meal he could never get tired of consuming.

With the way she was standing so close to him, he could feel the hard tips of her breasts pressing against his chest, and the heated juncture of her legs aroused his erection even more. And if those things weren't mind-wrenching enough, he pulled her closer to the fit of him, needing the intimacy of their bodies joined first in clothes and then without.

The thought of making love to her in his office suddenly sent a sexual urgency as strong as anything he'd ever encountered to fill him to capacity. And with a sharp hunger that could only be appeased one way, he lowered his head and greedily consumed her mouth, devouring its taste and texture. He felt her lips tremble beneath his, he knew the exact moment her tongue engaged in their sensuous play, something so powerfully erotic it made him growl deep in his throat. He knew the air conditioning was on and was working perfectly, yet he felt hot and the only way to cool off was to remove his clothes. Their clothes.

He broke off the kiss and quickly began unbuttoning his shirt, driven by graphic images flowing through his mind of just what he wanted to do to her. The thought made his lips curl into a smile.

"What are you smiling about?" she asked when he began removing his shoes and socks.

He glanced at her and chuckled. "Trust me, you don't want to know so I'd rather not tell you."

"But you will show me?" she asked when he began removing his pants.

He nodded. "Oh, yes, I will definitely show you."

Totally naked, he stood in front of her. He wanted to take her hard and fast, then slow and easy. He wanted to brand her. He wanted to …

Sensing he was suddenly about to lose it, he took a condom out of his wallet and quickly put it on before stepping closer to her to begin removing her clothes, appreciating the fact that she was helping. Otherwise he would have ripped them off her in his haste, his greed, his obsession.

When she stood before him completely nude, he knew that this was one immaculate woman, a woman who could turn him on like nobody's business. She was elegant and sexy, all rolled into one. He reached for her hand, took it in his and began walking backward toward his desk. He'd been fantasizing about taking her on it since the last time he'd brought her here. He could imagine her legs spread wide, with him standing between them and making love to her in a way that had his body hardening even more just thinking about it.

And they would be making memories. There would never be a time that he wouldn't enter his office without thinking about her, remembering what they had done in here, and remembering her being a part of him for this short while.

When they reached his desk he picked her up and sat her on it. A hot surge of desire rammed through him and he wanted his hands all over her, he wanted his body inside of her. He wanted it all. He reached out and let his fingers trace a path all over her, and pretended to write his name on her chest, stomach, thigh, everywhere.

And then he captured her mouth, sank into it with a hunger that was more intimate than any kiss he'd ever shared with a woman. She was consuming all of him, whether she intended to or not. Deliberate or accidental, he didn't care, she was doing it, taking him to a level that was physically exciting and emotionally draining all at the same time.

And when he gently leaned her back on the desk he spread her thighs and took his place between them—a place at the moment that was rightfully his. She looked beautiful with her hair a tousled mass on her head, flowing over her shoulders and falling in her face. He pushed the soft, curly strands back, not wanting anything to obliterate her vision. He wanted her to see every single thing he would do to her.

Her warm scent assailed him and he leaned forward and took her lips with an urgency, his tongue invading her mouth the way his erection was about to invade her body. Not wanting to wait any longer, knowing he couldn't even if he did, he pressed his engorged flesh against her and then when he felt her ultrawet heat, he eased it into her, clenching his teeth the deeper it went.

The sound of her moan pushed him into moving, stroking her body with his, thrusting in and out of her while holding her hips immobile. He made love to her with a primitive hunger that had him feeling every single sensation right down to his toes. Every stroke seemed keyed to perfect precision and his heart was pounding with each and every thrust.

He felt her shudder and his reaction to it was instantaneous. He was overtaken with pleasure so intense his body exploded in a million tiny rapturous pieces. Releasing the hold on her hips, he reached up and tangled his fingers in her hair as his entire body became one huge passionate mass. He pressed into her deeper still, when he felt the essence of him shooting into her womb as her flesh still continued to throb while his senses raged out of control. It was as if this part of her knew exactly what he needed and was giving it in full measure.

When she went limp, he somehow found strength to gather her into his arms to hold her, not wanting to let her go, wondering how he would do so when she left in two weeks. Not wanting to think about their parting, he picked her up and moved to sit behind the desk with her nestled protectively in his lap.

He glanced down at her. Her face wore the glow of a woman who'd just been made love to, a woman who had enjoyed the shared intimacy of a man. Not being able to stop himself from doing so, he reached out and began touching the swollen tips of her breasts. And when he noticed her breathing change, he leaned forward and took a tip into his mouth.

He wanted her again.

He lifted his head and met her gaze and his hand

began trailing down her body, seeking out certain parts of her. He heard her sharp intake of breath when his fingers touched the area between her legs.

"Had enough yet, baby?" he asked huskily in a low voice.

She clutched at his shoulders and whispered the one single word he wanted to hear. "No."

"Good."

He stood with her in his arms and headed toward the sofa. Tonight was their night. In the coming days the Garrisons would want to spend time with her before she returned home. But tonight was theirs and they would make memories to last.

Parker's secretary glanced up and gave Cassie a thoroughly curious look as she stood from her seat. "Mr. Garrison is expecting you and asked that I escort you to his office the moment you arrived, Ms. Garrison."

"Thank you."

Cassie followed the woman, knowing she had made the right decision in deciding to meet with Parker this morning alone. Regardless of her and Brandon's relationship, Parker was still his client.

She had talked to her own attorney and taken in all the advice he had given her. He had indicated he wanted to be included—whether in person or via conference call—in any business meetings that she and Parker conducted that included Brandon, as a way of making sure she was well-represented and not being compromised in any way. She came to the conclusion that things would be less complicated and more productive if she and Parker discussed things and tried to reach an agreement without any attorney involvement for now.

The secretary gave a courtesy knock on Parker's door before opening it and walking in. He turned from the window, which overlooked Biscayne Bay, and gazed at her. With his intense eyes on her she was struck again with just how much he looked like their father.

"You're staring."

She could feel herself blush with his comment. She noticed his secretary had left and closed the door behind her, and she was grateful for that. "Sorry, I can't get over just how much you look like Dad."

He chuckled slightly. "That's funny. I thought the same thing about you on Sunday. And I hadn't expected you to look so much like him."

The guard she put up was instinctive and immediate. Tilting her head back, she asked, "Who did you expect me to look like?"

He shrugged. "I don't know, probably more like your mother, a stranger, someone I really didn't have to relate to. But seeing you in the flesh forced me to admit something I've tried not to since the reading of Dad's will."

"Which is?"

"Admit that I do have another sister—one my father evidently cared for deeply to have done what he did," he said, while motioning to a chair for her to have a seat.

"But I'm a sister you'd rather do without," she said, accepting the seat.

He moved to take the chair behind his desk and grinned sheepishly. "Yes, but don't take it personal. I've felt the same way about Brittany and Brooke one time or another when they became too annoying. It was hard as hell being an oldest brother." And then he added thoughtfully, "As well as an oldest son."

A part of Cassie refused to believe her father had been so ruthlessly demanding of his firstborn. "Did Dad make things hard for you since you were the first?" she couldn't help but ask.

He seemed surprised by her question. "No, I made things hard on myself. I admired everything about him and wanted to be just like him. He was a high achiever in everything he did—sports, business, financial success. He was a man who was well-liked and admired by many. I never knew if I'd be able to grow up and fit his shoes, but God knows I always wanted to."

He paused then said, "But one thing about Dad was that he was fair, with all of us. At an early age we were encouraged to enter the family business and that's something none of us have regretted doing."

Cassie nodded. He had encouraged her to join the family business, as well. At sixteen she had worked part-time for the hotel and when she had graduated from college he had given her the responsibility of managing it. It had been a huge responsibility for a twenty-two-year-old, but he had told her time and time again how much faith he had in her abilities.

And she hadn't wanted to let him down…just like Parker had probably grown up not wanting to let him down as well. Did he assume that since their father hadn't left him the bigger share of the pie that somehow he had?

"Dad was proud of you, Parker," she decided to say.

She saw the glint of surprise that shone in his eyes. "He discussed us with you?" he asked.

"Of course, considering the circumstances, he wasn't able to tell all of you about me, but I've always known about the five of you. He used to talk about what a wonderful job you were doing and that he had no qualms about turning the running of the entire company over to you one day."

Parker leaned back in his chair and Cassie felt him study her intently while building a steeple with his fingers. "If what you're saying is true then why are you and I sharing controlling interest?"

Cassie smiled. His arrogance was returning. "Because I'm good at what I do just like you're good at what you do. He knew both of our strengths, as well as our weaknesses, and although you can't quite grasp it now, I think he figured that over the long run, the two of us would work together for the betterment of the company. You even admitted that Dad was a fair man."

"Yes, but—"

"But nothing, Parker," she said, leaning forward in her seat. "He was a good and fair man, point blank. And I'm sure Brandon has told you by now that I won't sell my portion of the controlling shares."

"Yes, he did say that," Parker said, and Cassie smiled at the tightening of his lips. There was no doubt in her mind that Parker Garrison was used to having his way, something she hoped his wife Anna was working diligently to break him out of.

"I'm here to make you another offer, one we can both live with," she said.

The look in his eyes said he doubted it. "And what offer is that?"

"Like I've told you, the Garrison Grand-Bahamas

is my main concern, but I won't give away a gift Dad gave to me. However, I will agree to sign my voting proxy over to you with the understanding that you inform me of all business decisions, not for my approval but just to keep me in the loop on things, since I'll be in the Bahamas."

Cassie saw the protective shield that lined the covering of his gaze when he asked, "Are you saying you won't sell the controlling shares but you'll give them to me by way of proxy?"

"Yes, that is exactly what I am saying. Since I'm signing them over to you it will basically mean the same thing, except I retain ownership. Yet it removes me from having to provide my feedback and vote on every single business decision you make."

The room got quiet and she saw the protective shield become a suspicious one when he asked, "Why? Why would you do that?"

A quiet smile touched the corners of her lips. "Because I believed Dad all those times when he said you were one of the most astute business-minded persons that he knew, and because I also believe that you will do what you think is best for the company and keep Dad's legacy alive for the future generation of Garrisons."

She could tell for a moment that Parker didn't know what to say. And then finally he said, "Thank you."

She nodded as she stood. "No need to thank me, Parker. Have Brandon draw up the papers for me to sign before I leave."

He stood, as well. "You'll be here another week, right?" he asked.

"That had been my original plan but I've decided to leave at the end of the week. I haven't told Brandon of my change in plans. I will tell him tonight."

Parker came from around the desk to stand in front of her. "Cassie, Brandon is a good man. In addition to being my attorney, he's also someone that I consider a good friend. The reason he did what he did when he came to the Bahamas—"

She waved off his words. "I know, he explained it all to me. Although I was furious at the time I'm okay now." *I'm also very much in love,* she couldn't add.

"Anna and I would like to have you over for dinner before you leave. Will you be free Wednesday night?"

Cassie smiled, feeling good that she and Parker had formed a truce. She thought about all the other dinner engagements she had scheduled that week with Stephen, Adam, Brittany and Brooke, and said, "Yes, I'd like that and Wednesday night will be fine. Thanks, Parker."

Brandon sat looking at Cassie on the dance floor with Stephen, who had dropped by to see her before she left for the Bahamas. Tonight was her last night in Miami and he had brought her to Estate, Adam's night-club. It was Thursday night, which Adam had long ago designated as ladies' night.

Brandon had been surprised and disappointed when Cassie had told him a few nights ago that she would be leaving Miami a week earlier than she had originally planned. He had come close to asking her not to go, to stay with him, and not just for another week but for always. But then he remembered what she had said about the Bahamas being her home and not ever wanting to live anywhere else. Little did she know that when she left she would be taking a piece of his heart right along with her.

"Brandon, got a minute?"

He glanced up at Adam. "Sure, what's up?"

Adam straddled the chair across from him and glanced around as if to make sure no one was in close listening range. He then met Brandon's curious gaze. "I've decided to run for president of the Miami Business Council."

Brandon smiled. "That's great, Adam. Congratulations."

Adam grinned. "Thanks, but don't congratulate me yet. Already there's a problem."

Brandon raised a curious brow. "What kind of a problem?" Both he and Adam had been members of Miami's elite Business Council for years, and evidently Adam felt it was time to step up and take control. Brandon saw no problem with him doing that. Like his brothers, Adam was an astute businessman and the success of Estate could attest to that.

"Some of the older members, those with clout, aren't taking me seriously. They see me as a single man who is a notorious playboy, and since I work in the entertainment field, they also see me as someone not suited to lead the business council."

Brandon stared over at Adam. Unfortunately, he could imagine the older, more conservative members saying such a thing to Adam. "So what are you going to do?"

"One of the things that someone suggested that I do is easy."

"Which is?"

Adam smiled. "Work on expanding the club's clientele beyond the young, rich and famous. But the other suggestion won't be so easy."

"And what was that suggestion?" Brandon asked, hearing a hint of despair in his best friend's voice.

"To clean up my playboy image it was suggested that I find a wife."

Brandon blinked. "A wife?"

Adam nodded. "Yes, a wife. So what do you think?"

Brandon frowned. "I think you should tell whoever told you that to go to hell."

"Be serious, Brandon."

Brandon's frown deepened. "I am serious." He then sighed as he leaned back in his chair. "Okay, what if you did consider doing something like that? What woman will marry you just to help you advance your career that way?"

Then before Adam could respond, Brandon said, "Don't bother answering that. For a split second I forgot your last name is Garrison. You'll have all kind of greedy-minded, money-hungry women lining up at your door in droves. Is that the type of woman you'd want to be strapped to for the rest of your life?"

"It won't be for the rest of my life. I'm only looking at one year, possibly two. I want a woman who'll agree to my terms. We can get a divorce at the end of that time."

Brandon took a sip of his wine and asked, "And where do you intend to find such a woman?"

Adam shrugged. "I don't know. Do you have any ideas?"

Brandon chuckled and said the first name that came to his mind. "What about Paula Franklin?"

Adam glared at him. "Don't even think it."

Paula had first made a play for Parker a few years ago and when Parker hadn't shown her any interest, she had moved on to Stephen. Stephen had avoided her worse than Parker had, and she'd finally turned her sights on Adam, determined to hook up with a Garrison.

Adam had been forewarned about Paula from Parker and Stephen and hadn't been surprised when she had shown up at the club one night, ready to make a play for him and willing to do just about anything to succeed. When he had refused her advances, she had all but stalked him for a few weeks until he had threatened her with possible harassment charges.

Brandon gazed at him thoughtfully for a minute and then smiled and said, "Okay then, what about Lauryn Lowes?"

Adam gave Brandon a look that said he'd lost his mind. "Straight-laced Lauryn Lowes?"

Brandon ignored the look and said, "Yes, that's the one. You have to admit she's a picture of propriety, something those older, conservative members would want in a wife for you, so consider it a plus. And she's not bad-looking, either."

Brandon's words got Adam to thinking. "Lauryn Lowes."

Brandon stood and clapped Adam on the shoulder. "Yes, Lauryn Lowes. And while you're giving that some thought, I'm going to steal my girl from Stephen for a dance."

"Umm, that's interesting," Adam said, looking at him.

Brandon paused. "What is?"

"That you consider Cassie *your girl*. If she's your

girl then why is she leaving town tomorrow to return to the Bahamas?"

Brandon frowned. "She said she needed to go. What was I supposed to do? Hold her hostage? The Bahamas is her home, Adam, and she doesn't want to live anywhere else. She told me that a few days after we met."

"Have you given her a reason to change her mind?" Adam asked. "Maybe it's all been for show and you really don't care about her as much as I assumed you did. But if I cared for a woman, I mean really cared for one—although mind you, I don't—I would do whatever it took to make sure we were together, and nothing, not even the Atlantic Ocean, would be able to keep us apart." Before Brandon could say anything, Adam got out the chair and walked away.

Brandon took that same chair and sat, thinking about what Adam had said and his mind began racing. Although Cassie never said she loved him, a part of him had always felt that she did whenever they made love. She would always give herself to him, totally and completely.

And although he had never told her how he felt, he knew in his heart that he loved her, as well. He loved her and he wanted her, but he didn't want her to be with him in Miami if she wasn't going to be happy. Besides, her hotel was in the islands. It wasn't like she could fly over there every day for work.

He suddenly rolled his eyes when a thought flickered through his mind and he wondered why he hadn't thought of it before. He took a few moments to consider the idea, evaluate the possibility and then decided he would make it work. He laughed out loud, pretty pleased with himself.

"What's wrong with you?"

Brandon looked into Stephen's concerned face. Instead of answering he glanced around and asked, "Where's Cassie?"

"She's still out there dancing," Stephen responded, sitting down at the table. "Another song came on and this guy asked her to dance."

"And you let her?" Brandon asked, actually feeling a muscle tick in his jaw.

The sharp tone of his voice actually surprised Stephen. "Was I supposed to stop her or something?" When Brandon didn't respond, Stephen asked, "What's going on, Brandon?"

Brandon searched the dance crowd for a glimpse of Cassie. He saw her dancing to a slow song in another man's arms.

"Brandon?"

He glanced across the table at Stephen. "What?"

"I asked what's wrong with you?"

Brandon stood again. "Nothing's wrong with me. In fact at this moment everything is right with me. I think I'll go dance with Cassie."

Stephen shook his head, hiding his grin. "She's already dancing with someone."

"Too bad."

Like a man on a mission, Brandon crossed the room and tapped the man dancing with Cassie on the shoulder. The man turned and glared at Brandon, but instead of saying anything, he graciously moved away.

As soon as he did so, Brandon took hold of Cassie's hand and pulled her into his arms.

She glanced up at him and smiled. "The song is almost over so you didn't have to cut in, Brandon."

"Yes, I did."

"Why?"

"Because I didn't like the thought of another man touching you."

This was the first time she'd ever witnessed Brandon in a possessive mood and she made a half-hearted attempt at a chuckle. "And why would that bother you?"

"Because it does."

"Why?"

The song had ended and when others began returning to their tables, he took a firm hold of Cassie's hand and said, "Come on, let's take a walk."

They went outside and moments later they walked down a group of steps that led to the beach. Cassie paused long enough to remove her sandals. Her heart was beating fast and furious within her chest. Why had Brandon gotten all possessive and jealous all of a sudden? Could it mean that he cared for her more than she'd thought? A degree of hope stirred within her chest.

She decided to break the silence surrounding them. The only sound was the waves hitting the shoreline. "Estate is a very nice club."

Brandon stopped walking and she did likewise. She looked up at him and the bright lights from all the businesses on the beach lit his features. He was staring at her, his dark gaze intense. "I didn't bring you out here to talk about Adam's club," he said.

She looked away for a moment, across the span of the Atlantic Ocean, trying to maintain her composure. When she turned back to him, glancing up at him through her lashes, she asked, "Then what did you bring me out here to talk about, Brandon?"

For a brief moment Brandon couldn't speak. All he could do was stare at Cassie while his throat was constricted. Slowly expelling a deep breath, he said, "Our feelings for each other."

She met his gaze. "Our feelings for each other?" she repeated.

"Yes. I want to know where do you see our relationship going after you leave here tomorrow?"

As far as Cassie was concerned, the question he asked wasn't a difficult one to answer. "Nowhere."

Brandon tried to ignore the sharp pain that touched his chest. "And why do you think that?"

"Why would I not think that?" she responded in an irritated tone. "You've never said anything about continuing a relationship with me."

She was right. He hadn't. "I was afraid to," he said honestly.

She met his gaze. "Afraid? Why?"

"I knew what you told me weeks ago about how much you loved your homeland and not ever wanting to leave the island again to live anywhere else. I knew I could never take you away from that so I couldn't see a future for us. I was giving in to our demise too easily. But now I know what my heart is saying."

She studied his intense features before asking in a soft voice. "And what is your heart saying, Brandon?"

He took hold of her hand and brought her closer to

him and then placed that same hand on his chest and over his heart. "Listen."

She felt the gentle, timely thump beneath her hand and then heard him when he said, "It's a continuous beat that's saying over and over again, I, Brandon Jarrett Washington, love Cassie Sinclair-Garrison, with all my heart, soul and mind. Don't you hear it, sweetheart?"

Cassie fought back the tears that threatened to fall, "Yes, I can hear it now."

He smiled. "And do you also hear the beats that are saying that I want to marry you, make you my wife and give you my babies."

She chuckled. "No, I don't hear those ones."

"Well the beats are there, drumming it out loud and clear. What do you think? And before you answer I want you to know that I have no intention of asking you to leave the island to move here to accomplish any of those things."

She lifted a brow. "You're anticipating a long-distance marriage?"

He heard the disappointment in her voice. She was probably remembering the sort of absences her parents had endured. "Not hardly. I plan for us to live together in the Bahamas as man and wife and I will use my private plane to commute to Miami each day. It's less than a thirty-minute flight. Some people spend more time than that on the highways to get to work."

Her heart was filled with even more love when she said, "You would do that for me?"

He smiled and took his thumb to touch the dimple in her chin. "I would do that for us. I love you and I am determined to make things work." He then leaned down and captured her mouth with his and she shuddered under the mastery of his kiss. Moments later, when he pulled back, she was left quivering.

"Are you with me, sweetheart?"

She reached up and placed a palm to his cheek and smiled. "All the way."

He tightened his hold on her hand and tugged her in another direction. "Where are you taking me?" she asked, almost out of breath."

"Home. And I think we need to cancel your flight in the morning. My heart is beating out plenty of other words that you need to listen to, so I think you need to stick around."

Cassie smiled, totally satisfied that her heart belonged only to this man, and that it would always be that way. "Yes, I think I will stick around for another week after all, especially since my heart has a few special beats of its own, as well, Mr. Washington. And they are beating just for you."

\* \* \* \* \*

Melita had been expecting a chaste quick kiss of the generic variety. But this kiss with Sully was the kind that sparked a dying flame to life. The kind of kiss you can't plan for. The kind of kiss memories are built on.

The memory of her murdered lover, Nemo, came to her then and she made a starved little noise in the back of her throat. She raised her arms and threaded her fingers through Sully's hair, pulled him closer. Felt his body settle, then melt into her.

In that instant her hunger for him grew, and his for her. She pressed herself to him with more urgency, and he responded in kind.

Melita came out of her kiss-induced memory of Nemo with a start. "Wait a minute." She pushed Sully away from her. "You bastard!"

She spit two nasty words at him in Greek, then wiped his kiss from her lips.

"I thought you deserved some solid proof that I'm still in one piece." He started for the door. "The clock's ticking, honey. Come on, let's get out of here."

"That's it? You sucker me into kissing you, and that's all you have to say?"

"I'm sorry. How's that?"

He didn't sound sorry in the least. "You're—"

"Getting out of this godforsaken prison cell. Stop whining and let's go."

"Not if I was being shot at sunrise. Go. You deserve whatever you get if you walk out that door."

He turned back. "Freedom is what I'm going to get."

"A second of freedom before the guards in the hall shoot you." She jammed her hands on her hips. "And to think I was worried about you."

"If you're staying behind, it's no skin off my ass."

"Wait! What about our deal?"

"You just said you're not coming. Make up your mind."

"Have you forgotten we need a boat?"

"How could I? You keep harping on it."

"I'm not going without a boat. And those guards out there aren't going to just let you walk out of here. You need me and we need a plan."

"I already have a plan. I'm getting out of here. That's the plan."

"I should have realized that you never intended to take me with you from the very beginning. You're a liar and a coward."

Of everything she had read, there was nothing in

Sully Paxton's file that hinted he was a coward, but it was the one word that seemed to register in that one-track mind of his. The look he nailed her with a second later was pure venom.

He came at her so quickly she didn't have time to get out of his way. "You know I'm not a coward."

"Prove it. Give me until dawn. I need one more night to put everything in place before we leave the island."

"You're asking me to stay in this cell one more night...and trust you?"

"Yes."

He snorted. "Yesterday you knew they were planning to harm me, but instead of doing something about it you went to bed and never gave me a second thought. Suppose tonight you do the same. By tomorrow I might damn well be in my grave."

"Okay, I screwed up. I won't do it again." Melita sucked in a ragged breath. "I can't leave this minute. Dawn, Sully. Wait until dawn." When he looked as if he was about to say no, she pleaded, "Please wait for me."

"You're asking a lot. The door's open now. I would be a fool to hang around here and trust that you'll be back."

"What you can trust is that I want off this island as badly as you do, and you're my only hope."

"I must be crazy."

"Is that a yes?"

"Dammit!" He turned his back on her. Swore twice more.

"You won't be sorry."

He turned around. "I already am. How about we seal this new deal?"

He was staring at her lips. Suddenly Melita knew what he expected. "We already sealed it."

"One more. You enjoyed it. Admit it."

"I enjoyed it because I was kissing someone else."

He laughed. "That's a good one."

"It's true. It might have been your lips, but it wasn't you I was kissing."

"If that's your excuse for wanting to kiss me, then—"

"I was kissing Nemo."

"What's a nemo?"

Melita gave Sully a look that clearly told him that he was trespassing on sacred ground. She was about to enforce it with a warning when a voice in the hall jerked them both to attention.

She bolted away from the wall. "Get back in bed. Hurry. I'll be here before dawn."

She didn't reach the door before he snagged her arm, pulled her up against him and planted a kiss on her lips that took her completely by surprise.

When he released her, he said, "If you're confused about who just kissed you, the name's Sully. I'll be here waiting at dawn. Don't be late."

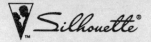

# Romantic
# SUSPENSE

## *Sparked by Danger, Fueled by Passion.*

Onyxx agent Sully Paxton's only chance of
survival lies in the hands of his enemy's daughter
Melita Krizova. He doesn't know he's a pawn in the
beautiful island girl's own plan for escape. Can
they survive their ruses and their fiery attraction?

*Look for the next installment in the
Spy Games miniseries,*

# *Sleeping with Danger*
# by Wendy Rosnau

*Available November 2007 wherever you buy books.*

# ATHENA FORCE

*Heart-pounding romance and thrilling adventure.*

**History repeats itself...unless she can stop it.**

Investigative reporter Winter Archer is thrown into writing
a biography of Athena Academy's founder. But someone
out there will stop at nothing—not even murder—to
ensure that long-buried secrets remain hidden.

## ATHENA FORCE

Will the women of Athena unravel Arachne's powerful
web of blackmail and death...or succumb to their
enemies' deadly secrets?

### Look for

# VENDETTA

### by *Meredith Fletcher*

*Available November
wherever you buy books.*

# *Mediterranean* NIGHTS™

*Not everything is above board
on Alexandra's Dream!*

*Enjoy plenty of secrets, drama and sensuality
in the latest from Mediterranean Nights.*

**Coming in November 2007...**

# BELOW DECK

*by*

## *Dorien Kelly*

Determined to protect her young son,
widow Mei Lin Wang keeps him hidden
aboard *Alexandra's Dream* under cover of
her job. But life gets extremely complicated
when the ship's security officer, Gideon Dayan,
is piqued by the mystery surrounding this
beautiful, haunted woman....

# REQUEST YOUR FREE BOOKS!

## 2 FREE NOVELS PLUS 2 FREE GIFTS!

 **Silhouette® Desire®**

### Passionate, Powerful, Provocative!

# COMING NEXT MONTH

### #1831 SECRETS OF THE TYCOON'S BRIDE—
**Emilie Rose**
*The Garrisons*
This playboy needs a wife and deems his accountant the perfect bride-to-be…until her scandalous past is revealed.

### #1832 SOLD INTO MARRIAGE—Ann Major
Can a wealthy Texan stick to his end of the bargain when he beds the very woman he's vowed to blackmail?

### #1833 CHRISTMAS IN HIS ROYAL BED—Heidi Betts
A scorned debutante discovers that the prince who hired her is the same man who wants to make her his royal mistress.

### #1834 PLAYBOY'S RUTHLESS PAYBACK—
**Laura Wright**
*No Ring Required*
His plan for revenge meant seducing his rival's innocent daughter. But *is* she as innocent as he thinks?

### #1835 THE DESERT BRIDE OF AL ZAYED—
**Tessa Radley**
*Billionaire Heirs*
She decided her secret marriage to the sheik must end…just as he declared the time has come to produce his heir.

### #1836 THE BILLIONAIRE WHO BOUGHT CHRISTMAS—
**Barbara Dunlop**
To save his family's fortune, the billionaire tricked his grandfather's gold-digging fiancée into marriage. Now he discovers he's wed the wrong woman!